SEA
BREEZE
ACADEMY

ALSO BY BRYANT A. LONEY

Exodus in Confluence

—

A NOVELLA

To Hear the Ocean Sigh

—

A NOVEL

Take Me to the Cat

—

A NOVEL

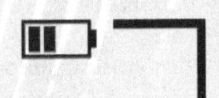

SEA BREEZE ACADEMY

As seen by

BRYANT A. LONEY

VERONA BOOKSELLERS

TULSA

Published by VERONA BOOKSELLERS

Contact info@VeronaBooksellers.com for information about special discounts for bulk purchases. The author does not in any way endorse, condone, or encourage engaging in any conduct depicted in this story. The publisher does not assume responsibility over any website and website content not owned by the publisher, as well as for changes that occur after publication.

Lyrics from "Night Train" (written by Nick Burton and Douglas Fournet) used by permission of The Side Effects, copyright © 2014. All rights reserved.

Publisher's Cataloging-in-Publication Data

Names: Loney, Bryant A., author.
Title: Sea Breeze Academy / Bryant A. Loney
Description: Tulsa, OK: Verona Booksellers, 2018.
Identifiers: LCCN 2017918970
    ISBN 978-0-9971700-2-3
    Summary: A group of boarding school teens in season five of a Cali-based sitcom begin to realize they are in a TV show.

Subjects: LCSH Boarding schools—Fiction. | Friendship—Fiction. | Situational comedies (Television programs)—Fiction. | Interpersonal relationships—Fiction. | Coming of age—Fiction. | High school—Fiction. | California—Fiction. | Satire. | BISAC YOUNG ADULT FICTION / General Classification: LCC PZ7.L8443 Se 2018 | [Fic]—dc23

Published in Tulsa, Oklahoma, U.S.A. by Verona Booksellers
"Where Books Are Still Sold!" www.VeronaBooksellers.com

Cover design by Deranged Doctor Design
Book design by Inkstain Design Studio
First Edition: June 2018
10 9 8 7 6 5 4 3 2 1

*To the kids raised by the television,
rotten brains 'n' all. Welcome back.*

Thought you were the only one,
Thought that we would never break up,
Take you home to meet my parents.

Fall in love with me,
I'd sweep you off your feet,
And then we'd go and marry each other.

But I am through with being a lover,
And I am through with being a fighter.
So settle down and simmer out
And take the night train out of town.

—THE SIDE EFFECTS, "Night Train"

I created myself to death.

—LAURA MORIARTY

PREVIOUSLY ON
SEA BREEZE ACADEMY...

After a semester of dating drama, Brooklyn "Rook" Rivers decided not to attend the junior prom with her friends in the season four finale of *Sea Breeze Academy*—until BFF Matthew Flynn surprised her by returning to campus after months away in Alaska!

The gang deserved their night of fun: Virgo and Chris planned a successful prom, Liss and Rhys declared their love for each other, and Brooklyn and Matthew shared their first kiss after years of just being friends. Now Matthew's got plans for the rest of the semester, and they all center around the girl of his dreams. But a relationship with Brooklyn might just be harder than he ever imagined...

What's next for this group of teens at their elite boarding school on the California coast? Grab your surfboard and catch Brooklyn and Matthew in season five of *Sea Breeze Academy*, where lots of sunshine and a gorgeous beach make going to school a perfect breeze!

EPISODES

SEA BREEZE ACADEMY

1. Hey Darren?
2. Go ahead.
1. Hey I'd like 57B done as well.
2. Yeah I'm sure he'll do both.
1. OK I'll make sure he does it. Thanks bud.

"HOVERBOARD BLUES"

Dean Fischer bans all hoverboards from campus after multiple accidents. The gang seeks to overturn the banning.

Another perfect day in Southern California. Matthew, eyes closed, relaxes in a hammock held up by two palm trees. In the background is the Pacific Ocean. The wind is light.

There's a whirring sound. Matthew opens his eyes to see Chris—his black best friend—farther off, moving closer, though Chris's legs do not move. Curious, Matthew leans forward.

Chris says, "Check it out! Early birthday gift!" He floats around the palm trees. Matthew cranes his neck to follow. "My mom got it for my birthday next week. Kind of wish she'd sent it last month during the half-priced coffee craze. This baby's gonna make the nine a.m. walks to pre-calc a whole lot easier."

Matthew hangs his feet over the hammock. Chris is standing on what seems to be a self-balancing scooter of sorts.

Matthew says, "Your birthday's next week?"

Chris stops circling. "Oh, hardy-har-har. You do this every year. We've been roommates since the sixth grade! So I know you know my birthday is always right after—look, will you just appreciate the hoverboard for me?"

"That's a, uh, hoverboard?" Matthew asks. "Aren't those supposed to, you know... hover?"

"Unfortunately, real life is not like what you see on TV. Still didn't stop Rhys from buying one as soon as he saw mine—one-hour delivery and everything."

Rhys rolls up on his own hoverboard and says, "Hey, Matthew. 'Sup, Chris. Lame hoverboard you got there. Mine's the YOTRAIL Blazer V-9™ model." He grins the sort of grin only a wealthy and obnoxious white dude can give. "Mom got it for me."

Chris says, "Yeah, well, my momma's a veterinarian. Yours is in movies. And there's nothing wrong with my hoverboard!"

Rhys says, "Yeah, but does it play music? Does it get WiFi?"

Matthew says, "Why would your scooter need to play music?"

"In case I want to make a cool entrance, all right? And this is not *just* a scooter. The Blazer® is a personal transportation device that at the bare minimum cuts the time I need to take from our dorm to Parssinen Hall by eight minutes. Eight! Do you know what I can do with eight minutes of quality alone time?"

Matthew says, "You mean other than stare at yourself in the mirror?"

Chris says, "I don't think I *want* to know what he can do with himself in eight minutes."

Matthew and Chris laugh.

Rhys says, "Okay, one, how dare you; two, that's not appropriate; three, it's my job to make those kinds of jokes; four, this hair doesn't fix itself; and five—"

Rhys shoves Chris off his hoverboard. Rhys then picks up Chris's board and uses his own to drive around the palm trees. Chris gets up and chases after Rhys, and yet Chris just can't seem to catch him.

Chris says, "Man, when I get my hoverboard back, I'm gonna find that hairbrush of yours and—"

Rhys reverses to face Chris. Rhys then accelerates, the hoverboard whirring loudly. Chris's eyes widen, and then it's Rhys chasing Chris around the palms. Matthew rolls his eyes, though he's smiling all the same. He begins to pack up his hammock.

Matthew says, "Well, if you fellas will excuse me, I'm going to go find somewhere else to nap."

Rhys says, "Tell Brooklyn we said hi!"

Chris says, "Tell Brooklyn to *get the dean!*"

Rhys laughs. "Where's campus police when you need 'em?"

Matthew shakes his head, still smiling at his friends' antics as he leaves with his hammock under one arm. Chris and Rhys's arguing grows fainter as he descends the hill toward campus, the great blue of the ocean behind him, and also, it's time for a commercial.

* * *

Back at Sea Breeze Academy, Matthew sees aspiring actress Virgo working the outdoor SBA coffee cart in Mintz Plaza. He sets his hammock down on a bench and joins the line of cheery-eyed teens. When it's Matthew's turn, Virgo smiles.

VIRGO

Hey, Matthew. (Eyeing the hammock.) You here to loiter or buy a cappuccino?

MATTHEW

(Laughing.) I'll have whatever that last guy just had.

VIRGO

You do *not* want what the last guy just had. (Stretching.) But if you're not gonna get something, why don't you buy *me* a coffee so I can spend this time talking without the line getting angry? (Leaning forward.) I get half off.

MATTHEW

Ha. Fine.

Matthew hands Virgo a five. She snatches it.

VIRGO

Great! (Digging around in her cart.) Have you seen Brooklyn today? I think she was looking for you.

MATTHEW

No, Rook hasn't texted me since earlier. She was getting something from mail services—

VIRGO

Male services? Already? Haven't you both been dating officially for, like, a week now?

MATTHEW

Oh, ha-ha. You're *so* funny.

VIRGO

(Smiling.) And that comes free of charge.

There's a whirring as main-girl Brooklyn enters Mintz Plaza on a pink hoverboard of her own. She spots Matthew and Virgo and then waves at them.

BROOKLYN

Hey, guys! Look what I got!

Brooklyn jolts forward a foot. She puts her arms out to balance herself. Matthew steps toward her.

BROOKLYN (cont.)

No, no, don't worry, I got this, I—

The hoverboard lurches out from under Brooklyn's feet, knocking her off and onto her side. Matthew and Virgo rush over, to the annoyance of the line. The hoverboard drives itself into a wall and stops there.

MATTHEW

Rook! Are you okay?!

RANDOM BOY IN LINE

Hey, no barista means free coffee!

Virgo points a finger in his face.

VIRGO

Back off, buddy.

He does, hands out apologetically.

BROOKLYN

(Easing her way up.) I'm fine, I'm fine. Thanks. (Gesturing with her head.) Did you see my new Blazer®? I bought it for Chris's birthday as a surprise, but then his mom already got him a hoverboard, so I figured, why not use it myself?

MATTHEW

But yours is pink.

BROOKLYN

What's to say Chris can't have a pink hoverboard?

VIRGO

(Laughing.) Yeah, you saying boys can't drive pink?

MATTHEW

All right, all right, you got me there. (Smirking.) Is that what the school's advocating now? First it was simple stuff, like how girls can do anything boys can do, and guys can also be sensitive and emotional. But then it got serious when we started talking about divorce after Rhys's parents split up, or death when Mr. Wells passed away, and then—

Something explodes on the coffee cart.

VIRGO

Oh gosh, not during *my* shift!

Virgo leaves the pair to attend to the cart. The line applauds sarcastically.

BROOKLYN

Anyway, this is great news for us!

> Brooklyn quickly hugs Matthew. He tries to hold her, but Brooklyn lets go after a second.

MATTHEW

How so?

BROOKLYN

Well, you know, with you back from Alaska and all, our class schedules haven't really lined up. With the Blazer®, I can zip in and see you between classes more easily! More face time between us!

MATTHEW

(Laughing.) Are my texts not cute enough?

BROOKLYN

If by "cute" you mean those geology puns your teacher tells you all, then no, sorry.

MATTHEW

(Playfully.) What's wrong with that? Geology rocks!

BROOKLYN

(Groaning.) Oh my word.

MATTHEW

See, the key is to not take a pun too far. A pun is a wild creature. It depends on smell to navigate. Take a pun too far and it won't be able to find its way home. Save a life, save a pun, right?

Brooklyn smiles.

BROOKLYN

Right, got it. Don't take things too far. But anyway, can't you see how much easier our lives will be with a Blazer®? They're great! *VERTEX Magazine* Certified Best Product of Last Year!

MATTHEW

What?

Matthew waits, but no one says anything. They just smile. Matthew walks over to the wall and picks up Brooklyn's hoverboard. He frowns.

MATTHEW (cont.)

Chris and Rhys were arguing about their own hoverboards earlier. They were saying—

VIRGO

Oh, Dean Fischer, why hello there!

Dean Fischer, dressed sharp as always, enters the plaza with a briefcase in hand. Virgo steps in front of the cart and shoos the line away. The students begrudgingly step aside for the dean.

DEAN FISCHER

Good afternoon, Virgo. Hello, Brooklyn. And welcome back to SBA, Matthew. How was Alaska?

MATTHEW

Cold, sir.

DEAN FISCHER

I can imagine. It's nice to have you on campus again. Seems like you're a favorite around here. We missed that unusually freckled face of yours. (Beat.) It's not acne, is it? They have gel for that.

MATTHEW

Uh, no, sir. Just my face.

DEAN FISCHER

My son had awful acne. Looked like a pepperoni pizza! Or a blueberry muffin. And now I'm hungry. (To Virgo.) Can I get a banana bread muffin? And a brava macchiato?

VIRGO

Coming right up, sir!

> Dean Fischer hands Virgo his platinum credit card. While Virgo makes the drink, Matthew fidgets with Brooklyn's hoverboard. Dean Fischer notices.

DEAN FISCHER

Is that one of those hoverboard things? (Shaking his head.) I've read too many articles about the U.S. Consumer Product Safety Commission investigating reports of hoverboard-related fires and injuries. If the safety standards are still being reviewed, why do you kids insist on using those deathtraps? Already there've been several recalls! Whatever happened to simply walking and talking around outside with your peers?

BROOKLYN

Yeah, but this is a Blazer®, Dean Fischer. It's better—and safer—than the average brand.

DEAN FISCHER

That may be true, Brooklyn, and I usually trust your judgment more so than the other students'. But I'm just not sure anymore. I've seen too many kids slipping and landing on their backs, or driving themselves into a pool, or doing the stupidest of things on those hoverboards to try and impress their friends. You know the stairs in front of Parssinen Hall? Campus police saw a student try to ride a hoverboard off the top. The top! He's lucky he didn't break his neck! Think of the lawsuit, the paperwork!

BROOKLYN

But Dean Fischer—

DEAN FISCHER

We're a bike-friendly campus, Brooklyn. I just don't see why—

> There's shouting, followed by multiple whirring noises. In the distance are Chris and Rhys, racing on their hoverboards. Students move out of their way as the two tear up the plaza.

CHRIS

I'm gonna win! I'm gonna win!

RHYS

In no way am I buying you a coffee because you beat me!

CHRIS

I'm about to beat you with your hairbrush after what you said about my momma!

RHYS

You didn't let me finish!

CHRIS

And what were you going to say?!

RHYS

That she's a beautiful woman!

CHRIS

Oh. (Beat.) I'll tell her you said that.

MATTHEW

Guys, look out!

BROOKLYN

Dean Fischer!

> Chris and Rhys, not paying attention, look forward and then open their mouths in shock as they realize

they are about to run into the dean. Rhys jumps off his hoverboard in time, but Chris drives straight into the coffee cart, knocking it onto Dean Fischer as Matthew, Brooklyn, and Virgo leap out of the way.

The other students gasp.

Matthew and Brooklyn rush over to help lift the coffee cart off the dean. Several students film the incident with their phones.

MATTHEW

Dean Fischer, are you okay?!

DEAN FISCHER

(Out of breath.) Of course... of course I am not okay!

RHYS

That's a confusing way of phrasing it.

Matthew offers Dean Fischer his hand and pulls him up. Dean Fischer then glares at Rhys before looking around at the crowd, the overturned coffee cart, and the chaos that has become the plaza.

DEAN FISCHER

You! Coach Poole!

Coach Poole, walking by, looks to the dean.

DEAN FISCHER (cont.)

Give me your bullhorn!

COACH POOLE

My megaphone?

DEAN FISCHER

Whatever!

> Coach Poole looks down at his megaphone, sighs, and then hands it to the dean.

DEAN FISCHER (cont.)

Thank you. (Into the megaphone.) Attention, all SBA students! Effective immediately, Sea Breeze Academy prohibits the use, possession, or storage of all electronic skateboards, including self-balancing boards, hoverboards, and similar devices, in all academy buildings and on-campus housing facilities!

RHYS

But Dean Fischer, Chris wasn't on a Blazer®! The Blazer® is renowned for its safety f—!

> Dean Fischer cuts him off with another glare. Rhys shuts up.

DEAN FISCHER

As I was saying. (Into the megaphone.) Students with hoverboards are asked to remove the devices from campus by the end of the day. Possession of such a device will thereafter constitute a student conduct violation. We will follow the CPSC investigations closely and will reassess this policy once comprehensive safety standards have been developed. That is all.

Dean Fischer gives the megaphone back to Coach Poole, who cradles it. The dean rolls his eyes.

DEAN FISCHER (cont.)

Brooklyn, Matthew... Chris and Rhys... I suggest you consider renting some SBA bicycles, because by sunset today, those hoverboards of yours are banned from this campus. (To Virgo.) And somebody clean this mess!

Dean Fischer picks up his briefcase, walks away, stops, scrapes the muffin from his shoe, and then stomps off.

Coach Poole blows his whistle and tells everyone to move along. Virgo, crying, crouches down and begins to wipe up the spilled coffee. Chris and Rhys put away their hoverboards to help. From the swell of dramatic music and the worried looks Brooklyn and Matthew give each other, it must be time for a commercial.

* * *

Back at Sea Breeze Academy, the gang sits on a couple of couches in the girls' lounge in Dutton Suites: Brooklyn, Matthew, Virgo, Chris, Liss, and Rhys. Rhys has his arm around Liss, the quirk. Matthew and Brooklyn sit close to each other, but not too close. All drink from bottles of Whazz™.

VIRGO

Hey, how should I cut my hair? I have an appointment tomorrow, but with work and classes and prom last week, I haven't given it much thought.

CHRIS

With scissors. (Beat.) Probably.

> Brooklyn runs a tanned hand through her wavy blonde hair.

BROOKLYN

All I know is that full bangs are a must. And keep it dark and natural.

LISS

That reminds me: I think I discovered a better way to fix a bun that doesn't make my hair tangle as much.

VIRGO

Oh? Well, come on! What's the secret?

LISS

Basically, I just did the whole bottom and middle section into semi-small braids, but I left the top front part out—that way you can barely notice the braided sections, but it keeps my hair neater and distributes the weight of my hair better on my scalp.

RHYS

Babe, that's neat and everything, *really*, but can we all please focus on this dumb hoverboard ban?

BROOKLYN

Seriously. My Blazer® is the only way Matthew and I'll be able to see each other during the week. (Sighing.) This is so suckish. And at the end of our junior year too. How am I supposed to use my Blazer® now?

CHRIS

You could ride at night, when it's dark.

BROOKLYN

Oh gee, if only my classes weren't during the day.

MATTHEW

Rhys, Liss, when did you both become a, uhh… thing? Like, a couple.

VIRGO

They'd been secretly dating for, like, two or three months. They masked it by pretending to hate each other even more than usual.

CHRIS

A *lot* happened while you were in Alaska.

RHYS

And now Liss is my little honeybee.

LISS

And Rhys is my handsome snuggie woogems.

MATTHEW

Good God.

Rhys and Liss proceed to rub their noses together affectionately. Matthew looks longingly to Brooklyn. Her mind is clearly elsewhere.

BROOKLYN

Dean Fischer just doesn't know how awesome the Blazer® really is. If we could convince him somehow...

MATTHEW

Liss, couldn't you invent something like a hoverboard for Rook? (Laughing.) Maybe a teleportation device?

LISS

Oh. I don't really do that kind of engineering anymore. I'm more interested in art history.

MATTHEW

But you... you're so good at physics and biology and chemistry and technology! That's been your passion since we first met. You invented a *germ* last semester. What happened?

VIRGO

She changed her mind, kind of like how she wears contacts now. Are you not respecting a woman's agency?

BROOKLYN

Her right to choose what she does with her future?

VIRGO

And yet Liss still kept the lab rats. Bleh.

BROOKLYN

Yeah, and I don't really go by "Rook" anymore, since it was a derivative of "rookie" meant to demean my status as an unknowing girl at a new school. I go by "Brooklyn" now.

CHRIS

Like I said, man, a *lot* happened while you were gone.

> Matthew stares at Brooklyn. She shifts in her seat, then takes a sip of orange Whazz™.

MATTHEW

But that's... that's not what I remember. That's not—

CHRIS

You know, maybe Dean Fischer has a point.

RHYS

Dude!

CHRIS

I'm serious! All those news reports and videos of hoverboards catching fire and people doing stupid stuff with 'em... (Beat.) Us included.

MATTHEW

I mean... yeah, that is a good reason to ban them. Safety for the students and all. If the CPSC says that they're dangerous—

> Brooklyn holds a finger to Matthew's lips.

BROOKLYN

Shh, shh. Baby, please. No offense, but you don't know what you're talking about.

RHYS

Besides, that's not exactly what kids want to hear. (Mockingly.) *Oh, it's totally okay if the dean takes your toys away because some government guys think your stuff is dangerous.* Like, really? How un-American. Where's your star-spangled freedom, man? Your love for Old Glory? Salute your independence!

BROOKLYN

Censorship is bad, Matthew. Taking away our Blazer® hoverboards is censorship.

MATTHEW

Huh? No, that's not… censorship.

BROOKLYN

Look, we just need to talk to Dean Fischer. Then he'll see how efficient, reliable, and most important, how *safe* the Blazer® hoverboards are.

MATTHEW

What's with the registered trademark thing?

Brooklyn smiles, a bright spark in her eyes.

BROOKLYN

Come on. I think I have an idea. But first, let's go find the dean. And Rhys, bring your credit card.

RHYS

Always do.

Brooklyn takes Matthew by the hand and leads him off the couch. The rest of the gang follow. The dramatic music swells once more as the setting sun casts an orange glow over the now-empty lounge, which can only mean it's time for a commercial.

* * *

Back at Sea Breeze Academy, Brooklyn, Matthew, Virgo, Chris, Liss, and Rhys walk to the administration offices. There, over two dozen students are protesting outside Dean Fischer's office windows. They chant and hold signs with sayings such as "Free the hoverboards!" and "Give us back our rides!" and "We love Whazz™ sports drinks!" Coach Poole stands between the protestors and the entrance. The signs wave gently in the soft coastal breeze.

In front of the crowd stands *SBA News* reporter and senior Denzel Davis with a microphone and camera crew. News music plays.

DENZEL

Good evening, Sea Breeze Academy. We hope you're enjoying your weekend. (Motioning to the crowd.) I am standing in front of a group of protesters seeking an overturn of the hoverboard ban imposed by Dean Fischer earlier today after students Chris Carmichael and Rhys Underwood ran into the dean while racing on their hoverboards through Mintz Plaza. The crash caused an SBA coffee cart to fall over onto the dean, trapping him momentarily. Student-filmed footage of the event is shown on your screen now. Dean Fischer cited the current United States Consumer Product Safety Commission investigations into hoverboards as his reasoning for the ban, stating that at sunset today, quote, "Possession of such a device will thereafter constitute a student conduct violation," end quote. Dean Fischer has yet to address the protesters, and campus police are nowhere to be seen. Reporting to you live from the G. M. Jenkins Administration Offices, I'm Denzel Davis. This is *SBA News*.

> The music fades, the camera crew leaves, and Denzel packs up his stuff. Chris walks over to him. They fist-bump.

CHRIS

Hey, Denzel. Thanks for the shout-out. What's happening?

DENZEL

No problem, brother. And you know, the usual. Protests like these happen at least once a semester, from Dean Fischer replacing the vending machines with healthy alternatives, to girls not being allowed to wear tank tops on campus—and in Southern California, no less. That last one was changed thanks to you and your friends, but it's strange, 'cause Dean Fischer would normally make a statement by now. He's been quiet in there.

BROOKLYN

It's Coach Poole. We need to get past him somehow.

CHRIS

I got this. Matthew, help me out.

> Chris and Matthew separate from the group and approach Coach Poole, who stands with his arms crossed in front of the administration building's entrance.

COACH POOLE

Carmichael. Flynn. Can't let you boys in there. Sorry.

CHRIS

Oh, we're just stopping by. (Fanning himself.) Whew! Sure is hot out. What's the temperature?

> Matthew takes out his phone.

MATTHEW

Ninety-one degrees.

CHRIS

Boy. And these kids don't have anything to drink, do they? Seems a bit irresponsible for the head coach of the basketball, volleyball, baseball, track, wrestling, golf, tennis, surfing, and water polo teams to let these kids stand in the heat without staying hydrated.

MATTHEW

Uhh, yeah! You should probably get them some water, Coach.

CHRIS

Whazz^{TM} would also work.

MATTHEW

But... that has caffeine in it. (Beat.) Like, I know it's a sports drink, but Liss found caffeinated stimulants in it that one time last year. Remember? During finals week? (Beat.) There was an explosion?

CHRIS

Things explode all the time.

COACH POOLE

Okay, caffeinated beverages do help when it comes to staying hydrated. People often think that they don't because caffeine is a diuretic, but the effects of a normal, healthy amount of caffeine are not going to significantly contribute to water loss—as long as you don't overdo it. So yes, Whazz™ counts. They also sponsor the school. But if you do drink a ton of caffeinated drinks, yeah, you should supplement with water. (Sighing.) So much of the public health industry in this country is controlled by the corporations that benefit most from our ignorance. It's sad, really. We believe and teach so many lies to our youth.

CHRIS

So are you going to get these folks some Whazz™ or what?

COACH POOLE

All right, Carmichael. You win. I'll see what I can do.

> Coach Poole walks away. Chris gives the gang a thumbs-up, then he, Brooklyn, Matthew, Virgo, Liss, and Rhys sneak around the protesters and into the administration building.
>
> Dean Fischer, a bandage over his forehead, paces

around the desk in his office on the ground floor. The blinds are lowered, yet the sun still casts a soft red yellow into the room. When he sees the gang, Dean Fischer scowls at them.

DEAN FISCHER

I knew I shouldn't have sent my secretary home early. She wants to be at her daughter's *big orchestra concert*, ooohh, fancy, look at me, playing the cello. And look what happens!

Dean Fischer raises the blinds. The group of protesters has grown substantially. Brooklyn steps forward.

BROOKLYN

Dean Fischer, we're sorry for the crowd. It's just that we believe the ban is unfair, is all.

DEAN FISCHER

Well, it's nice that you think that, Brooklyn, but this? (Pointing.) This is disrupting. And it's embarrassing for the school! What am I supposed to do when so many accidents are happening because of those... those ridiculous hoverboards!

BROOKLYN

But that's the thing—you're right in that some hoverboards are dangerous, but the Blazer® is totally safe!

DEAN FISCHER

For all I care, the Blazer® could file my tax returns, and I still wouldn't allow it on this campus!

RHYS

Why would a self-balancing scooter need to do your taxes?

Dean Fischer glares at Rhys.

RHYS (cont.)

Anyway, we thought you might feel this way, 'cause it's hard to grasp how truly awesome the Blazer® is without trying one for yourself. (Grinning.) So that's why we got you a little something.

A postal worker in uniform walks into the room with a large box in her hands.

POSTAL WORKER

The door was unlocked. (Checking the label.) I have a package for a Mr. Charles Fischer?

DEAN FISCHER

(Sighing.) That would be me.

The postal worker hands him the box, then leaves. Dean Fischer opens it and pulls out a shiny red hoverboard. He sets it on the desk.

RHYS

Thank you, one-hour delivery. (Beat. To the group.) Wait, I thought "Dean" was his first name.

DEAN FISCHER

I can't believe this. After I specifically banned them from this campus, you kids got me a hoverboard?!

BROOKLYN

But sir, that's not just a hoverboard.

VIRGO

It's a Blazer®!

LISS

VERTEX Magazine Certified Best Product of Last Year!

MATTHEW

How do you all know these things?

> The protesters' chanting grows louder from outside. They
> begin banging on the windows and throwing tomatoes.

DEAN FISCHER

This is absurd. Tomatoes?! Where are they getting fresh produce?!

> Dean Fischer stomps over to the windows and flings
> them open. The crowd steps back.

DEAN FISCHER (cont.)

You all, listen to me! Hey! Listen up! I am in charge of this school!
And when I say something is banned, I mean it! (Taking a breath.) If
you want to request a change in policy, you may do so either through
your dorm advisor or via our website at SeaBreezeAcademy dot com.
But what we *do not* and *will not* tolerate at this educational institution
is *vandalism by tomatoes* and a disruption of campus life by needless

protesting! This is a fire hazard, people!

Another tomato is hurled at the dean.

RANDOM GIRL IN CROWD

Free the hoverboards!

RANDOM BOY IN CROWD

Give us back our rides!

SMALL BOY IN CROWD

Yeah, Dean Fischer! Fuck you!

> Everyone gasps, staring at the small boy. He covers his mouth, his eyes wide, looking around frantically. The crowd slowly backs away from him. Coach Poole sets down the cases of Whazz^{TM} and stares, shocked.

MATTHEW

Oh my God.

> Men in suits walk into the scene with clipboards and earpieces. Two of the larger ones each take an arm of the boy and lift him off the ground. He does not squirm or attempt to fight them. They carry him away and place him in the back of a white SBA utility van farther off. It drives elsewhere.
>
> Dean Fischer looks down at his dress shoes. Rhys puts an arm around Liss, and Virgo starts cracking her knuckles. Chris shifts around awkwardly, but Brooklyn

doesn't move. She doesn't even breathe.

Matthew sees a couple of seagulls flying over campus toward the Pacific, where the orange of the horizon has faded into purple. He looks next at the hoverboard, then to the crowd, then Dean Fischer, then Brooklyn. Matthew slowly takes her hand. Brooklyn lets him.

The low rumble from the van is heard no more. A bird's eye view of Sea Breeze Academy, and then the credits roll.

1. Hello Brandon?
2. Hello.
1. Hey buddy, did you and Arthur update the E-7 pack?
2. Uhhhh no, I don't think we need to update it anymore.
1. 10-4.

"WELCOME TO SBA: PART 1"

Transfer student Brooklyn Rivers makes new friends on her first day at Sea Breeze Academy, a spacious, open-air, multi-acre boarding school in Southern California.

A clear sunny day in Southern California. Winter break is over, and with the new year comes fresh faces to the prestigious Sea Breeze Academy. Mellow rock music plays as dorm advisors help newcomers to campus, seasoned students walk around in shorts and tank tops, and a compact red rental car slowly rolls up to the curb beside the administration building.

Inside the car is Brooklyn Rivers, a pale girl with blonde hair, blue eyes, and a wide smile on her face. In the driver's seat is Brooklyn's mother, Mrs. Rivers, who has darker hair and early wrinkles. Brooklyn tries to steady a digital camera in her shaking hands so she can capture the scenery, which isn't Malibu exactly, but similar.

BROOKLYN RIVERS

Mom, look at this school! It's gorgeous! There are palm trees, like, literally everywhere!

MRS. RIVERS

If there were palm trees *literally* all over, then this place would be a jungle, hon, not a boarding school. And one of the highest-ranked in the country, I might add. (Smiling.) Bet you here they would have taught you the difference between "literally" and "figuratively" by this point.

BROOKLYN

(Laughing.) Oh, Mom, come on. It's just that I'm excited, is all.

MRS. RIVERS

I'm serious! This school is known worldwide for its professors and faculty. You're going to receive a fantastic education here—I know it.

BROOKLYN

Yep! Great education, better vocabulary... maybe a tan...

MRS. RIVERS

More like a sunburn if you're not careful.

> Brooklyn looks over to her mother and laughs. Mrs. Rivers grins and joins her. Brooklyn then opens the car door slightly, but before she can leave, Mrs. Rivers reaches over her to gently shut it.

BROOKLYN

Mom, what are you doing—?

MRS. RIVERS

Just... take a moment. Sit here with me.

Mrs. Rivers leans back and closes her eyes. Brooklyn watches her mother, confused.

MRS. RIVERS (cont.)

As soon as you open that door, this becomes real, and then I won't see you till the summer. (Choking up.) You're my little girl, Brooklyn.

BROOKLYN

Hey, Mom, it's okay.

Brooklyn puts an arm around Mrs. Rivers, who leans into it, softly crying.

BROOKLYN (cont.)

I'll call you, you know that. And I'll email you every day.

MRS. RIVERS

I just... what if I forgot something? Like, to teach you how to remove a stain, or how to shine your shoes, how to use chopsticks, arrange flowers, how to shovel snow—

BROOKLYN

Shovel snow? Here?

MRS. RIVERS

You know what I mean!

BROOKLYN

Mom, please, there are dorm advisors for that. And if not, well, I have world-renowned professors, right?

MRS. RIVERS

Still... (Sighing.) When you're sad, you can't hug a professor.

BROOKLYN

It's the second week of January. June will be here before we know it.

MRS. RIVERS

And I expect you to know the difference between "literally" and "figuratively" by then. I mean it. Now, well, give me a kiss before I start crying again.

> Brooklyn laughs and then kisses her mother on the cheek. Mrs. Rivers smiles, teary-eyed, before bending down to pop the trunk. Brooklyn then exits the car and walks behind it to pull out three large suitcases, which she then lugs over to the sidewalk. Mrs. Rivers rolls down the window.

MRS. RIVERS (cont.)

You gonna need any help with those, sweetie?

> Up ahead are several students in orange polos holding up signs with different names on them. Brooklyn spots her name, then lowers her eyes to the person twirling it around: Chris Carmichael, a black guy with short hair and an athletic build. When he's not messing with the sign, Chris is laughing and chatting with the other SBA class representatives beside him.

BROOKLYN

I think... I think my tour guide's up ahead. I'll be right back.

Brooklyn brushes down her sequin-hemmed denim skirt. She takes a deep breath. She then walks across the path lined with palm trees and benches, weaving her way between tables for fundraisers and volunteer services. One boy struggles to sling a heavy duffel over his shoulder while a girl strolls by with a surfboard under her arm. Two kids race each other on bikes and two others on skateboards. In a grand field with impeccably cut grass, some boys with sun-stained hair are playing tackle football, and some loungers are spread out on blankets and enjoying snacks. A coffee-drinking couple laugh and playfully shove each other. The midday sun is gentle. The Pacific air is just right.

Chris sees Brooklyn approaching, stops talking to the dude next to him, and then smiles with a genuine enthusiasm that Brooklyn can't help appreciating.

CHRIS CARMICHAEL

Hey there! Are you Brooklyn?

Chris holds out a hand for her to shake. She does so.

BROOKLYN

Uh, yes! That would be me.

CHRIS

Awesome! Welcome to Sea Breeze Academy. My name's Chris. I'm also a ninth grader in the upper school like you, so if you got any questions about your class schedule or which courses to take, totally let me know. As a student ambassador, I'm your liaison your entire first semester here, so anything you need, I got you, girl.

BROOKLYN

(Laughing.) Thank you. I'll probably need all the help I can get.

CHRIS

Speaking of which, are those your bags over there? By the red car?

Brooklyn nods.

CHRIS (cont.)

Hey, Siddiq! Yo! Brogan! Mind helping a fella out?

Two basketball players in orange polos, Siddiq and Brogan, look from Chris to the luggage by the rental, nod, and then do some quick pushups before heading over to the car.

CHRIS (cont.)

(To Brooklyn.) What dorm are you in?

BROOKLYN

(Pulling out a paper from her back pocket.) Uhhh, Dutton Suites, I think—

CHRIS

Take her stuff to Dutton Suites!

BROOKLYN

Room a hundred and two.

CHRIS

Room one-oh-two!

>   Siddiq and Brogan give a thumbs-up each.

CHRIS (cont.)

Thank you, sirs! (To Brooklyn.) You ready to hit it?

BROOKLYN

Yeah, just let me say bye to my mom first.

CHRIS

Of course, of course. Take your time. I'll be here.

>   Brooklyn fast-walks over to the car, where Mrs. Rivers
>   stands, blowing her nose into a tissue. Brooklyn hugs
>   her mother, and Mrs. Rivers returns the embrace.

MRS. RIVERS

You be careful, Brooklyn, and drink lots of water. If you die from heat exhaustion, I swear, the dogs will never forgive you.

BROOKLYN

We're from Oklahoma, remember? I think I know how to keep myself hydrated.

MRS. RIVERS

I literally hope you do. (Smiling.) And be sure to say hi to your cousin for me! Daisy's a seventh grader this year. Oh, and Brooklyn? (Beat.) No boys.

BROOKLYN

Oh, Mom!

> Brooklyn and Mrs. Rivers hug once more. As Siddiq and Brogan haul away Brooklyn's belongings, she waves to her mother one last time before returning to Chris. When Brooklyn looks back, Mrs. Rivers is driving away from campus and then turning left onto the Pacific Coast Highway. Brooklyn smiles.

CHRIS

You ready?

> She nods.

CHRIS (cont.)

Walk with me.

> Brooklyn and Chris stroll across the main campus at a leisurely pace, with Chris pointing out various buildings as they pass them by. They step around different games

of Frisbee and old friends catching up.

CHRIS (cont.)

Up in the highlands is the chapel—sometimes you'll hear the bells ring—while the lakes, gym, amphitheater, and our two auditoriums are down below. You probably saw them on your way to the admin building. Now over there is Zhang Hall—that's where you'll take any foreign language classes. It also has the tables with the best view of the ocean, so definitely eat lunch there if you can. Little ways past that, here, is Jepperson Hall—that's mostly, um, psychology, sociology, you know, those sorts of deals. All the buildings here have a rectangular... *modern* design. Basically, you know it's SBA when you come across a set of white buildings with red roofs.

BROOKLYN

I can't believe I can see the beach from here. This place is like a fancy resort, with the little villas and everything!

> Chris laughs.

CHRIS

Something like that, sure. It really is a nice place. I've been asked before, like, if I won the lottery, would I quit school. And I'm like, no way, dude, SBA is awesome! I love it here. Just because we're learning shouldn't mean we have to suffer. You feel?

BROOKLYN

Definitely.

CHRIS

So I guess what I'm saying is... don't wait for someone to give you permission. Explore your interests these next few years and truly take advantage of all the opportunities this school provides you. You're only as young as you'll ever be, you know? (Smiling.) What do you want to study?

BROOKLYN

Me? Oh, well, I like to write. So writing, I guess.

CHRIS

You should definitely see about working for *SBA News*—like, we have our own facility, channel, webcast, everything. The top reporter's name is Denzel Davis. You'll find him all over this place. He's only a grade above us too. I can introduce you both if you'd like.

BROOKLYN

Thanks, but I meant writing more as in... screenwriting or playwriting. I'd like to write and direct my own TV show one day.

CHRIS

Hey, that's awesome! Virgo Torres—I think she's your roommate in one-oh-two—um, she ran a book club last semester, and we read some cool plays in there. *Waiting for Godot, Life is a Dream, Lysistrata...* She wants to be an actress. Should talk to her about it sometime. Oh! This building's Parssinen Hall, where the English department is located. If you're into writing, you'll spend a majority of your time either here or at the library. Or in the lounge at Dutton Suites, I suppose, if it's not game night. To get there, you'll walk through Mintz Plaza, our food court, which is just through here—

Brooklyn accidentally runs into a tanned dude in an oxford shirt, khaki shorts, and boat shoes without socks. The guy, Rhys Underwood, quickly steps back and whips off his aviators. His eyes flash green with anger.

BROOKLYN

Whoa, I am so sorry—

RHYS UNDERWOOD

Hey, crazy chick, watch it! This outfit costs more than your dorm room!

Brooklyn puts her hands on her hips.

BROOKLYN

Oh, *my bad*, I didn't know this school had classes on how to be a jerk, 'cause you're sure acing that one.

CHRIS

Brooklyn—

BROOKLYN

And maybe if you weren't wearing sunglasses, you'd be able to *watch where you're going!*

CHRIS

It was an accident, Rhys.

RHYS

Gaah, you stupid little—

Rhys stops himself. He looks down at the aviators he's holding. He puts them on.

RHYS (cont.)

Um, yeah. Sorry.

Rhys runs his fingers through his bleached-blond hair, then quickly walks away.

BROOKLYN

Well, that was… was weird. (Shaking her head.) Pretty boy always an idiot like that?

CHRIS

(Finger-quoting.) "Pretty boy" is one of my roommates, and unfortunately, yes, sometimes. Rhys—rhymes with "Greece"—kind of had a rough end to last semester before the break. It's a, uh, long story. For another time. (Looking off.) Speaking of roommates…

On the edge of a lavish fountain in the middle of Mintz Plaza sits Matthew Flynn, a skinny white guy with dark hair, freckles, and bushy eyebrows. Matthew's at the end of a comic book, its pages up to his face, his head moving from side to side as he reads. The fountain shoots water high into the air.

CHRIS (cont.)

Yo, Matthew! Come meet the new girl!

Matthew looks up at Brooklyn's eyes, cool like the ocean breeze, which seem to complement everything from the soft slope of her nose to her delicate shoulders. She smiles, warm and dimple-decorated. Matthew rises to his feet too quickly, slips, and immediately falls into the fountain.

BROOKLYN

Oh my God!

Brooklyn and Chris rush over to help Matthew, who is soaked and looks a bit perplexed. Chris offers Matthew his hand, and Matthew spits out a couple of pennies back into the fountain before accepting it. Chris pulls him up and out.

CHRIS

Dude, you okay?!

MATTHEW FLYNN

Oh yeah, yeah, totally! No, it was, um, it's hot out here, anyway. Was actually wanting to go for a swim later, so that, uhh, worked out nicely. Yeah.

Matthew looks at Brooklyn, then smiles nervously, still in a joyous daze. He holds out his hand.

MATTHEW (cont.)

Hi, I'm Matthew.

BROOKLYN

(Smiling again.) Brooklyn.

She takes it and shakes it.

CHRIS

What were you reading there?

MATTHEW

Oh, I was, umm, I was reading the newest, uh, *Captain Canary*. He's one of the lesser-known superheroes. (Beat.) It's kind of stupid actually…

BROOKLYN

No, that sounds neat. Really!

Matthew beams.

BROOKLYN (cont.)

It's cool to be, like, passionate about something, you know? Plus someone wrote that comic, illustrated it, so at the very least you're supporting the creators. It's entertainment. No shame in that. (Glancing up at the fountain.) What kind of a superhero is Captain Canary?

MATTHEW

(Grinning.) His powers are avian. He's half-bird, half-human.

CHRIS

What the heck does that even mean?

MATTHEW

Exactly what it sounds like?

> Brooklyn smiles. Matthew leans over to look into the
> fountain, reaches in, and then fishes out the comic.

MATTHEW (cont.)

Ah well. Guess it doesn't matter now.

BROOKLYN

Oh gosh, I'm so sorry. I didn't mean for—

MATTHEW

What, this old thing? No, no, it's fine! I just finished. They're too
distracting, anyway, *comic books*. Now I won't procrastinate as much.
You probably saved my French grade. See?

> Matthew throws the comic over his shoulder, back into
> the fountain.

MATTHEW (cont.)

Tomber dans les pommes! Faire l'andouille!

> Brooklyn giggles while Chris shakes his head.

CHRIS

Whatever you say, Captain Canary. Hope you enjoyed the bird bath.
(Shrugging.) Well, anyway, good seeing you, roomie, but I gotta get
Brooklyn to her dorm room—

MATTHEW

Oh yeah. Cool. (To Brooklyn.) You're new to campus, right? A transfer student? Where from?

BROOKLYN

Oklahoma.

MATTHEW

Oklahoma?

CHRIS

Yeah, man. It's, like, Diet Texas.

BROOKLYN

(Smiling.) More or less.

Matthew laughs.

MATTHEW

All right, Okie cowgirl. See you around?

BROOKLYN

Sure thing, Captain Canary.

MATTHEW

Aack, gross, don't call me that.

BROOKLYN

(Laughing.) Then don't call *me* that!

CHRIS

(Taking Brooklyn by the shoulder.) Come on.

> Chris pulls Brooklyn away from the fountain, turning around briefly to salute Matthew. Brooklyn flashes Matthew a smile and then waves him goodbye. Matthew waves back.
>
> Away from Mintz Plaza, Chris and Brooklyn continue walking normally uphill.

BROOKLYN

He seems nice.

CHRIS

Yeah, he's a good kid.

BROOKLYN

Better than that other one.

> Chris stops in front of a building.

CHRIS

Tell me, are you single? Leave anyone behind in Oklahomaland?

> Brooklyn raises an eyebrow.

BROOKLYN

I'm not dating anyone, no.

CHRIS

Then you are really gonna like it here. Don't worry. Rhys and Matthew are only two of the hundreds of dudes on this campus. So let me be the first to say... (Gesturing toward a grand view of the campus below them and the sun setting over the Pacific.) Welcome to SBA.

> The sky is now a deep orange with blazing streaks of pink, and the ocean a blue serene. A light wind brushes against the palm leaves, scattering gulls and fireflies. A tennis match draws to a close. Both parties shake hands. A volleyball game has just begun. Folk music plays. In the distance, fireworks. This is Sea Breeze Academy.

BROOKLYN

Wow... that's all I can say, really.

CHRIS

It's nice. *Better be*, given our tuition.

> The two admire their campus for another moment. The wind picks up slightly. Brooklyn shivers.

CHRIS (cont.)

Well, this is where I leave you. This is Dutton Suites.

> Chris points. Brooklyn looks.

BROOKLYN

It's... just like every other building.

CHRIS

Sure, except that you live here. Plus you get a swell view of the coast. And the tennis courts! The boys practice in the a.m., so that's nice to wake up to. Uh, for you, I mean. (Beat.) I dunno. (Stretching his arms.) And like I said, anything you need, I'm either practicing with the SBA band or at my dorm room in Wright Suites. My cell phone number should be in that letter they sent you.

BROOKLYN

Hey, thank you, I appreciate all this. (Running a hand through her hair.) I just feel bad about Matthew and his comic.

CHRIS

(Smiling.) Well, I'll let him know you're thinking of him. Anyway, see you tonight at the dean's open house?

BROOKLYN

I got the email about that, but what's—?

CHRIS

It's a New Year's tradition that the dean invites everyone to his place for an evening of eating, dancing, meeting new people, and just having an all-around good time. Dress code is semi-formal. The event's totally optional, but it's always a lot of fun. (Nudging Brooklyn.) Plus free food, am I right?

Brooklyn laughs.

BROOKLYN

Yeah, I'll see you there.

CHRIS

Cool. The shuttles meet by the administration building—that's where you were dropped off—and the last one leaves at seven. Now go meet your roommates!

BROOKLYN

Okay, okay! Golly Moses, I will!

Chris stares at her blankly.

BROOKLYN (cont.)

Yeah, you heard what I said!

Chris laughs, shaking his head, and then walks off. Brooklyn smiles to herself before turning around to take in the sight, sound, and smell of the shimmering blue sea once more. She then goes up to the building's entrance and grips the handle. She pulls. With a sigh of relief, Brooklyn steps inside her new home, and also, it's time for a commercial.

* * *

Back at Sea Breeze Academy, Brooklyn walks through the Dutton Suites lounge—past all the couches, the Foosball machine, the smoothie bar, the giant flat-screen TV, and a donation box for the local fire department—to get to the front desk. There sits Sage Harris, a tall, pretty woman in her late twenties with dark skin and curly hair. Sage is watching an *SBA News* interview with the dean. As she notices Brooklyn, Sage smiles and stands to meet her.

SAGE HARRIS

Hey there! Are you one of the new students?

BROOKLYN

Hi, yeah, I am. My name's, uh, Brooklyn. Rivers.

Sage scans a sheet of paper on the desk.

SAGE

Yep! Here you are. Room one-oh-two.

Sage picks up a key from the rack behind her and hands it to Brooklyn. Sage then moves around the desk and gestures with her head for Brooklyn to follow. They walk.

SAGE (cont.)

All the dorms are down the hall, with the laundry room and kitchen on the other side. My name's Sage, by the way. Officially "Mrs. Harris," but we're informal around here, so just Sage is fine. I'm your student life counselor, or SLC, with my husband being the SLC in Wright Suites, which is one of the boys' dorms. He and I actually went to school here maybe, oh, a decade ago. So if you have any questions for me about getting situated into campus life, what clubs to join, what the schedule is for the weekend shuttles to the beach, don't hesitate to ask. I'm here for you!

Sage stops in front of Room 102.

SAGE (cont.)

Believe it or not, I stayed in the room right next to yours my freshman year. (Knocking on the door.) Hey, Miki? Virgo? Come meet your new roommate.

> The door opens. Miki Mizushima, a tall, gorgeous Asian girl, stands next to Virgo Torres, a cute Hispanic girl with multicolored hair hidden beneath a turquoise spangled skullcap. There's a smile spread across Virgo's face as she bounces on the balls of her feet. Miki doesn't smile immediately, though she does extend a friendly hand.

MIKI MIZUSHIMA

Miki Mizushima. Welcome to paradise.

SAGE

Be nice!

BROOKLYN

(Shaking Miki's hand.) Brooklyn Rivers. Thank you.

VIRGO TORRES

Hey. I'm Victoria, but everybody here calls me Virgo because I act it.

SAGE

Now, Miki, didn't you say earlier some boys had dropped off Brooklyn's bags?

MIKI

Yeah, Siddiq and Brogan. (To Brooklyn.) We put your stuff on your bed, if that's cool.

BROOKLYN

Of course, yeah. Thank you.

SAGE

Well, I'll let you ladies get to talking. Make sure to figure out who's on kitchen duty for the week!

VIRGO

Thanks, Sage!

> Sage exits while Miki and Virgo step back inside. Brooklyn follows.
>
> The room is larger than Brooklyn expected, as evidenced by her shocked expression. The purple walls are covered with photographs of family and friends, movie posters, a line of paper-mache lanterns, and a few decorated letters that spell out HAPPINESS LIVES HERE. By the windows are three desks for studying, as well as a mini fridge. In the corner is a wicker basket holding bright beach towels and flip-flops. There's a single bed up against the right wall and a bunkbed opposite to it. The single bed, nightstand, and desk nearest to it are empty, save for Brooklyn's belongings and SBA bedsheets. The wall behind Brooklyn's bed is bare.

MIKI

We thought you might want the single bed to yourself. I'm on the bottom bunk, Virgo's up top.

Miki turns to face Brooklyn.

MIKI (cont.)

Are you allergic to anything?

BROOKLYN

Me? Um, no, not that I can think of.

MIKI

Oh, okay. Good. Some of the other girls and I baked cupcakes for the new transfer students, but then we got hungry, so, uhh, leftovers are in the fridge there.

She points.

MIKI (cont.)

I ask because *somebody*—

Miki glares at Virgo, who puts her hands angelically beneath her face as if to say, That's me!

MIKI (cont.)

—faked a peanut allergy when I made her brownies in the sixth grade.

Virgo twirls around.

VIRGO

What can I say? (In a posh voice.) *I'm an actor, darling!* (Play-serious.) "That has nuts in it? I'm allergic! I don't have my shots with me!"

> Virgo falls to the floor, spasming. Miki rolls her eyes and kicks Virgo in the side. Virgo breaks character and laughs from the ground.

MIKI

Yeah, not funny. Fatima legitimately has a peanut allergy. Zaley too! You scared me half to death, you freakish goober!

VIRGO

Yeah, and you almost poisoned me with your toxic peanuts!

> Miki kicks Virgo again. Virgo groans and eases her way back up.

VIRGO (cont.)

We also got you a succulent plant. It's on your bedside table. Its name is Gregg with two G's.

MIKI

Oh, so it's a boy plant then.

VIRGO

I dunno, let me ask.

> Virgo walks over and picks up the plant.

VIRGO (cont.)

Hey, Gregg. Are you a boy succulent or what?

> She waits. Virgo holds it up to her ear. She sets Gregg
> down.

VIRGO (cont.)

Gregg is shy.

BROOKLYN

Well, thank you both for welcoming me.

MIKI

Yeah, you like it here so far? The dorm... SBA... that gorgeous sunset...

BROOKLYN

Oh, totally. (Smiling.) I think I'll miss Oklahoma sunsets the most though.

> Brooklyn opens one of her bags and pulls out a
> photograph. She admires it momentarily, then places it on
> her nightstand. It's of an Oklahoma sunset: warm colors,
> powerlines, and dreams.

BROOKLYN (cont.)

Something about the colors there are... different—the oranges and purples and pinks and blues. Not better or anything, but unique. It's weird.

MIKI

What is?

BROOKLYN

Leaving the town I grew up in the past fourteen years—leaving that consistency behind. (Sighing.) I don't know...

VIRGO

Hey, don't worry. Being homesick is normal, but trust me, you'll get used to it here. Yeah, okay, midterms and finals *are* suckish—plus all the stairs around here, ughh—but come the end of the semester, you really won't want to leave, whether it be because of the friends you make or the beach or, hey, even the California rolls at Fukutsū, the sushi place on campus. And you'll have the calves of an Olympian by then for sure.

MIKI

Leg day every day.

VIRGO

We're honestly so blessed to be here.

MIKI

Yes, so abundantly blessed indeed. Want my advice? Go to class, focus on time management, and try to work out at least three days a week. It helps to destress, plus it's a good excuse to listen to music for an hour. Try to get good grades, but don't beat yourself up over bad ones. Reach to do better.

> Miki pulls over a chair from her desk and sits, facing Brooklyn. Virgo sits next to Miki on the carpet. Brooklyn leans against the bed.

MIKI (cont.)

But why'd you come here, anyway? What brings you away from all the Oklahoma farmland and horses and teepees and saloons—

VIRGO

Says the Canadian. (To Brooklyn.) First day I meet Miki, I ask if I should put on sunscreen. What does she tell me? "Well, if you're going oot, then there's no doot aboot it, eh?"

MIKI

You can't even tell anymore! I sound just like anybody else here! (Beat.) Besides, they only talk like that in Newfoundland.

        Brooklyn laughs.

BROOKLYN

Okay, and how many times have you surfed today, huh? What celebrities have you seen? You must be so rich, living in *totally radical* SoCal—

MIKI

Fine, fine, dumb question, I get it.

VIRGO

Yeah, Miss Ontario. Don't forget to say, "Sorry," eh?

MIKI

It's only a slight accent!

BROOKLYN

Same with me! *Tarnation!*

Virgo laughs, followed by Brooklyn. Miki smiles, then joins them.

BROOKLYN (cont.)

I don't know. I guess I'm trying to be more independent. I want to figure out who I am—to decide who I will be, what I stand for.

MIKI

That's good. You're definitely at the right school then.

Virgo scoots over to the mini fridge and takes out three cans of soda. She gives a blue one each to Miki and Brooklyn, then keeps a red one for herself. Virgo pulls the tab and raises the can.

VIRGO

To Sea Breeze Academy.

BROOKLYN

To SBA.

MIKI

Hear, hear.

They drink. Miki grimaces as she swallows the last mouthful.

MIKI (cont.)

Whew, that's the good stuff. (Placing her empty can on top of the fridge.) Okay. Time to put on a dress, do my hair, nails, and makeup, and then get you, Brooklyn, to the festivities tonight.

VIRGO

(Raising her drink triumphantly.) To the dean's house, mwahahaha!

MIKI

Mansion, more like.

> Miki reaches over by the door and grabs an oversized black purse.

MIKI (cont.)

This year's theme is "Winter Fiesta," so I'm expecting a *lot* of churros, hence the purse.

> Miki pats it. Virgo has moved over to the open closet. She holds up two pairs of shoes.

VIRGO

Flats or wedges? Miki, you're going with flats, right?

MIKI

Yeah right. (Checking her hair in the mirror.) I'm tall enough, but any opportunity to look down on know-it-all boys, I'll take it. Wedges all the way—

> Miki screams at her reflection. Virgo screams in response. Brooklyn jumps back.

VIRGO

Miki, what the heck?! Now *you're* scaring *me!*

MIKI

I have a pimple! Upper lip! Entirely under the surface—see?!

> Miki stomps over and lifts her head up for Virgo. Brooklyn looks as well.

VIRGO

At least it's cystic. No one can tell, really. It'll be dark, anyway.

BROOKLYN

I think I read somewhere that you could try putting an ice cube over it before applying concealer. The ice—it constricts the blood vessels a bit and brings down the inflammation. Makes the bump less noticeable.

> Miki gives Brooklyn a quick hug, then starts walking out.

MIKI

Ice it is. I'll go fetch a cube.

VIRGO

Pssh. I say you own it, girl. Let the pus flow free, my friend.

MIKI

(From out in the hall.) I just puked in my mouth, you goober!

> Virgo rushes over to the doorway.

VIRGO

Give your zit a name! Stick a googly eye over it!

MIKI

You're sick, Virgo! Sick!

VIRGO

Draw a fake mustache to cover it up! Dean Fischer'll sure love that.

MIKI

Bye! This is me gone!

Virgo turns to Brooklyn, grinning wide.

VIRGO

We're like fudge here. Mostly sweet... with a few nuts. (Beat.) Unless you're allergic, that is.

BROOKLYN

Which I'm not.

VIRGO

A witch I am not either. But Miki, oh yeah, totally. Now let's get ready. (Holding up the shoes again.) Flats or wedges?

Brooklyn opens her mouth to respond, though Virgo's already put on the flats. Brooklyn takes in her surroundings. She looks from Gregg the succulent to the SBA bedsheets, and then, last, at the outside view, grassed over in a dazzling green. Grounds workers load trays of food into the back of a van by the light of the streetlamps. A couple of hummingbirds float around a rosebush. There's the strumming of a guitar nearby and a friendly voice joining in for a song. The stars, magnificent as ever, swing and bow to the waves and campus in the waning light of dusk. Serenity. The calm.

Brooklyn's not sure what the future will hold—living on her own, making new friends, showing this school what she's really all about—but she knows it'll be amazing. So she smiles once more, and then the credits roll.

1. Hey say that again there bud?
2. I wanna isolate UV-12 and bypass it. I gotta do some instrumentation work on it.
1. OK. Just make sure you open the bypass first.

"VIRGO AT THE BOOKSTORE"

*Virgo and Brooklyn apply for jobs at the school bookstore.
Meanwhile, Chris and Rhys get lost on their class field trip
to the Saguaro National Forest.*

Another perfect day in Southern California. Brooklyn, Matthew, Chris, and Liss sit at a round, shaded lunch table outside Zhang Hall, overlooking the Pacific. They eat Indian food and drink palm-warmed bottles of Whazz™.

CHRIS
Ugh. I can't believe Mrs. Beach is making me research cactus plants for our desert unit in biology. I have to come up with thirty facts by tomorrow. There's nothing cool about cactuses!

BROOKLYN
I think you mean "cacti."

LISS
It's a foreign Latin ruling, so both are technically correct. Plus the scientific name for cacti is "Cactaceae." Cacti, as you know, primarily thrive in barren areas—mostly in the desert Southwest and in South

America. Basically, they don't proliferate in dark and damp climates. More interesting, a cactus can live up to three hundred years of age. So there's three facts for you!

CHRIS

Oh yeah, and did you know the largest cactus grew to be six inches tall? And that slicing a cactus open can bear the Golden Ticket to the Wonka Factory? Oh, and that cacti have a dual metabolism? Photosynthesis and *feasting on the blood of innocents*.

LISS

I know you're joking, but the genus of cacti *Cactoideae mortiferum* has survived for over a thousand years due to its consistent budding of the bloodflower, known for attracting hummingbirds. *Cactoideae mortiferum* is also known to emit a smell similar to that of rotting meat. That's because there's an animal trapped inside the cactus—the hummingbird. See, once a hummingbird falls prey to the toxic pollen, the bloodflower then changes its color from white to red. That's how the bloodflower cactus gets its blood, as well as its name.

> Brooklyn and Chris frown. Liss shrugs. The three turn to Matthew, who has been staring out at the ocean in the distance, wave after wave.

BROOKLYN

Matthew?

MATTHEW

Oh, sorry. Uhh, a cactus has three genders?

BROOKLYN

Too far. Try again.

MATTHEW

Ummm... they have spikes?

LISS

The spines of a cactus can either be spiked and pointy or like the hairs on your body. In fact—

MATTHEW

Wait, guys, what happened to that kid the other day at Dean Fischer's office?

CHRIS

What do you mean?

MATTHEW

You know... the small boy who was in the crowd protesting. He said... (Leaning in to whisper.) *He said a bad word.*

CHRIS

Yeeeeeaahhh, sorry, bro. Not sure what you're talking about there.

LISS

(Smirking.) I don't think Matthew knows how cactus facts are supposed to work.

MATTHEW

Guys, I'm serious. There were these men in suits, and they picked him up and dragged him off into a white van. We… just stood there.

CHRIS

I don't believe in biology.

BROOKLYN

And we respect your opinion.

> Rhys rolls up to the table on his hoverboard.

RHYS

There are two thousand species of cacti—that much I know.

MATTHEW

How are you on one those hoverboards? Dean Fischer banned them, remember?

RHYS

Dude, we've been over this. It's a Blazer®. And we talked Dean Fischer out of the ban. *You were there.*

MATTHEW

But the kid who said the bad word—

RHYS

It'll be fixed, all right? There are people for that. They'll work around it. Come on, man.

> Rhys picks up his hoverboard and scoots in beside Liss. Virgo walks up to the table with papers in her hands.

VIRGO

(Pouting.) I need help.

CHRIS

Grab some pine and sit.

Virgo settles next to Brooklyn.

BROOKLYN

This about your job hunt?

VIRGO

Yes! Ever since that fiasco with Dean Fischer and the coffee cart, I've been out of a gig, and these shoes don't pay for themselves!

Virgo raises her feet. Brooklyn and Liss admire Virgo's two-tone round-toed pumps. Chris strokes them momentarily before nodding his approval.

BROOKLYN

So what do you need our help with?

VIRGO

Well, I heard the SBA bookstore is hiring, right? So I printed off an application from the website. One of the interview questions is "What are your weaknesses?" Like, how do I answer that?

RHYS

Shouldn't be too hard, knowing you.

Virgo throws a piece of Matthew's food at Rhys's head. Rhys deflects.

CHRIS

You have to be honest, but make it also sound like it has benefits too. Like, for example, being slightly slower but more mindful of detail.

LISS

Exactly. Name the weakness, briefly give the steps you've already taken and will take to address it, and then refer to it as a growth point. Basically, don't beat around the bush.

RHYS

(Rolling his eyes.) No way. Look, you turn the question around and ask what *their* weaknesses are. Or be like me and say you don't have any. Actually, just stare at them. Say nothing. Establish dominance.

CHRIS

Man, what would you know?

LISS

Yeah, what Chris said. No offense, baby. At least he gets scholarship money from being in band. I tutor and Matthew worked in the cafeteria last year. You live off your mom's money.

RHYS

And there's nothing wrong with that!

LISS

Sure, but you're coming from a different, more *privileged* position than the rest of us. Virgo needs the cash.

BROOKLYN

I've also been looking for a job. (To Virgo.) Do you know how many positions the bookstore has available?

VIRGO

Yeah, two! I was gonna say you should totally apply with me! It'll be fun working together!

> Matthew scoffs, as if to ask why the bookstore is hiring with only five weeks left before summer, and what if the store can only hire one of them? Wouldn't the other be jealous—perhaps start some roommate drama?

LISS

Anyway, whatever you do, don't say you're a perfectionist. They've heard it before. And come up with smart questions to ask beforehand.

BROOKLYN

Matthew, any ideas?

MATTHEW

Oh. Well... for you specifically... you could tell them you occasionally try to please everyone at once, and sometimes that makes you feel like you take on too much responsibility.

> Brooklyn turns to Virgo. Virgo to Rhys. Rhys to Liss. Liss to Chris. Chris to Matthew. Matthew to Brooklyn. She holds his stare.

BROOKLYN

Umm. Too on-the-nose. (Beat.) Thanks though.

Brooklyn gives Matthew a quick kiss on the cheek. He blushes. Chris rises from his seat.

CHRIS

Right, so good luck to you both, but Rhys and I have to go pack for our field trip.

VIRGO

Where to?

RHYS

(Standing.) Mrs. Beach is taking our class to the Saguaro National Forest to look at some scorpions or red rocks or whatever.

BROOKLYN

Who knows—maybe you'll see a cactus in the wild!

CHRIS

Man, I hope not, with Liss all but confirming cactuses are hummingbird killers.

Everyone but Matthew laughs.

RHYS

Anyway, don't vomit on the interviewer! First impressions, you know!

VIRGO

Yeah, yeah. And you guys wear visors or something. It's hot! Stock up on Whazz™!

LISS

And watch out for bloodflowers!

> They laugh, and then Chris and Rhys leave the table. Matthew silently watches them from beside Brooklyn. From the concerned look she gives him to the way Virgo habitually crosses and then uncrosses her legs, it's obvious Matthew's behavior is making the gang uncomfortable, and also, it's time for a commercial.

* * *

> Back at Sea Breeze Academy, Matthew approaches the door to Room 102 in Dutton Suites. More important, Brooklyn and Virgo are interviewing together at the SBA bookstore, and Chris and Rhys are arriving with their class at the Saguaro National Forest.
>
> Away from the others, Matthew hesitates, then knocks twice. He waits. He is about to leave when the door opens. Liss stands on the other side, holding the handle.

LISS

Oh. Hey, Matthew. What's up?

MATTHEW

Sorry, I, uhh, was hoping to talk to Rook. Brooklyn, I mean. Her. My girlfriend.

LISS

Right. Well, she's with Virgo at the bookstore. They're both applying for the two open bookseller positions. Meanwhile, Chris and Rhys are out in the desert with their biology class. (Sighing.) So you and I are left with nothing to do. Except maybe study our stuff.

MATTHEW

That's right, yeah… huh. I guess I'll leave then.

LISS

(Slowly shutting the door.) All right, um, bye—

MATTHEW

Wait.

> Matthew looks around, sees no one, and then steps past Liss inside the room. A vintage yellow light pours in through the windows. He notices sand stuck permanently into the carpet. Matthew closes the door and then sits on the edge of Brooklyn's bed, which is cold and desolate.

LISS

So are we hanging out now, or…?

MATTHEW

What's going on? Like, the last day or so? I feel, I don't know, a bit lost, I guess. The campus is the same, but the people and all that's happened... You and Rhys, for example. Where did that come from? You couldn't be more different—him vaguely sexist, you being, well, intelligent...

LISS

He's a sweet guy. Rhys is so often typecast as this spoiled, narcissistic friend nobody likes—and yeah, he can be a real jerk—but you know what they say, opposites attracting. Like an ionic bond between two atoms.

MATTHEW

And all this happened while I was in Alaska?

LISS

(Laughing.) You say the campus isn't any different, but so much has changed. Like, did you know half the school is gay?

MATTHEW

Wait, you mean... (Looking around.) Gay as in...

LISS

Gay as in two guys holding hands or two girls kissing, yeah, that kind of gay. It's not that hard. Before, it could be inferred, or it was part of a joke, but now it's official. Rhys spent a whole day being angry about it, but thankfully, we were able to work out his internalized homophobia.

MATTHEW

Oh. Well, that's good... I suppose.

LISS

Then there was the bit about the new refugee students. That got some coverage. And there were smaller things, too, like the runaway girl, or Rhys gambling his dining dollars at secret parties, or even Chris's addiction to online gaming after you left. There was vandalism, learning disabilities, panic attacks, Brooklyn with her bipolar disorder... but yeah, half the campus being gay was a big deal. Racism too. Now Muslim girls are walking around in their hijabs. Non-Muslim girls too. Basically, half the school is now Muslim as well. So anyone you see, there's a good chance they're either gay or Muslim or both.

MATTHEW

Wow. I hadn't even noticed.

LISS

You will now. That's certainly the point.

MATTHEW

But that kid at the protest who said that thing to Dean Fischer. That was weird, right?

LISS

I don't know any more than you do.

MATTHEW

But I've never seen something like that! That's never happened before! (Beat.) Right?

LISS

We go to an expensive boarding school in SoCal. People come and go.

MATTHEW

Being dragged away is not "People come and go." Brooklyn's other roommate—that's coming and going. The tall girl. Miki. She and Brooklyn always fought.

LISS

Matthew, please, stop while you're ahead.

MATTHEW

Huh?

LISS

You're smarter than this. Miki Mizushima transferred out, yes, that's what happened.

MATTHEW

But that boy—

LISS

He probably transferred too. Maybe he got homesick.

MATTHEW

Five weeks before the school year's over with? It just doesn't add up.

LISS

Look, just stop, Matthew. Please. You're asking questions I can't give you answers to. This isn't... this isn't meant to be serious. Just lighthearted teen antics with any drama resolved by the end of the day. "Love, mystery, and adolescent angst," right? (Looking out the window.) I argued for you. We all did. You had a lot of support. (Turning to Matthew.) Don't mess this up. Please?

MATTHEW

Tell me the name of the boy.

LISS

We don't know. He was just some random kid with an SBA backpack and hoodie. He looked young—maybe an eighth or ninth grader? Daisy might've hung out with him.

MATTHEW

Oh my God, I totally forgot about Brooklyn's cousin! That's brilliant, Liss!

LISS

What can I say? I'm just your former gadgeteer genius, extraverted nerd, and brainy brunette. (Beat.) I'm still a brunette. Anyway, Daisy did become an artifact of sorts after last year.

She laughs.

LISS (cont.)

Seems like we've been focused a lot more on dating and social issues than schoolwork these days. It's... kind of sad, actually.

MATTHEW

At least you have your rats to cheer you up, right?

LISS

Yes. I'm just super stressed out all the time. The rats are too. And scared.

MATTHEW

Where are they—the rats? Shouldn't they be here? In your room?

      Liss's phone sounds. She checks the text.

LISS

It's Brooklyn and Virgo. I need to meet them at the bookstore. They got the job—*shocker*, I know—but try to act surprised when you see them.

MATTHEW

Yeah. Yeah, of course. I'm going to try to find Daisy.

LISS

She likes sushi, so you might check around Fukutsū, but don't take too long, all right? You have to be at the bookstore—

MATTHEW

Got it! Thanks!

      Matthew leaves the room and then pulls out his own phone. He checks it as he walks, his head angled down. Several students call out to him as he passes, though he doesn't appear to notice, and also, it's time for a commercial.

             * * *

Back at Sea Breeze Academy, Matthew walks through Mintz Plaza while looking for Brooklyn's ninth-grade cousin. More important, Brooklyn and Virgo are both working customer service for the SBA bookstore, and Chris and Rhys are officially lost.

In the plaza are a bunch of kids Matthew doesn't know. They all wear muted colors that blend into the background, and each is on their phone, their eyes fixed on their screens. The sun is high, and everything shimmers with the heat. Frustrated, Matthew sits on a bench near Fukutsū. He takes out his own phone instinctively. He then puts it away and sees Daisy with her back to him.

Matthew stands and walks over to her.

MATTHEW

Hey, Daisy—

Daisy turns around. She's wearing an orange crop top and denim shorts. She has a great tan. Her long blonde hair, like her older cousin's, falls strategically across her full breasts. Matthew can see traces of a black bra beneath her shirt.

DAISY

Matthew, hey! How are you?

Daisy hugs Matthew tight, thrusting her breasts against his chest. Matthew, embarrassed and roughly a head taller than Daisy, looks down and notices her generous cleavage. Matthew pulls out of her embrace.

MATTHEW

Hey, Daisy, it's, uhh, it's nice to see... you.

Daisy laughs.

DAISY

Great to see you too! Welcome back from Alaska! And now you're dating Brooke.

MATTHEW

And now I'm dating Brooke. (Looking around.) So, um, what about you? What've you been up to?

DAISY

Just hanging out, really. Me, Leith, and Brogan are part of a throuple.

MATTHEW

What's a throuple?

DAISY

Like, a couple but with three people instead of two.

MATTHEW

Oh. Wow. Okay, yeah, that's new. (Beat.) So is it you and Leith some of the days, and then Brogan and Leith on the others, or...?

DAISY

(Shrugging.) Nah. It's the three of us. Classes are suckish 'cause they only get in the way, but yeah, it's after class, before class... okay, sometimes even *in* class—

MATTHEW

Anyway! I just had a, uhh, quick question, and then you can go back to your triple-thing.

> Daisy laughs. She then saunters over to one of the benches and lies back, eyes closed, legs spread.

DAISY

What's your question?

> Matthew hesitates.

MATTHEW

Yeah, so, the other day, like, there was this protest outside Dean Fischer's office.

DAISY

Was this the one about hoverboards or full torsos needing to be covered at the fitness center?

MATTHEW

Hoverboards.

DAISY

Right. I saw that on *SBA News*.

MATTHEW

So you know about the ninth grader who got pulled away then? The one who said... well, a *bad word* to Dean Fischer.

DAISY

Yeah, he obviously didn't mean to say that. It just, like, happened. Like, how many times have you been caught up in the full heat of the moment—so passionate, so *intense*—when suddenly something just slipped out. And then you have to scramble to put it back in.

Matthew stares at her. Daisy blinks.

DAISY (cont.)

Ohhh, I remember. The covered-torso business was last month. Brooklyn was so mad 'cause, you know, she works out in a sports bra, and that Kallan dude, in one of those sideless tank tops. Brooke called it "absurd and archaic." Anyway, Brooklyn walked straight into the gym, demanded to speak to the person in charge, and after they finished talking, the policy was changed, just like that. Got deleted from the SBA website and everything.

MATTHEW

Hold up, who's Kallan? Do I know him?

DAISY

Huh? I thought this was about the guy who yelled at the dean.

MATTHEW

Oh, well, yeah.

DAISY

So anyway, the kid. He was one of the new refugee students from Yuran. He had a foreign name. Pulov? Yeah, Pulov was his name. We talked maybe once at a coffee cart.

MATTHEW

Awesome. Thank you, Daisy.

DAISY

Though to be honest, I'm not sure he was an actual refugee—I think he's from Vancouver. Like, he just looks Yurani. Anyway, you could probably check this year's yearbook to be sure. You can get them at the SBA bookstore.

MATTHEW

Hey, that's perfect! Brooklyn just got a job there!

DAISY

Oh, really? Good for her. And here I thought she was just another academic athlete—the pink-means-feminine, jack-of-all-trades, go-getter girl with a heart of gold.

Matthew stares blankly at Daisy. Daisy stares right back.

MATTHEW

Uhh, yeah, sure. Well, anyway, thanks for the info, but I should probably go meet up with her—

DAISY

Hey, Matthew, wait. (Smiling.) You wanna get sushi sometime? Catch up? We can talk about your time in the frozen north, throuples, our theories on Australia...

MATTHEW

What?

DAISY

Australia. I'm, like, ninety percent certain it's a myth. Have you ever been? Doesn't it just sound fake? Like, literally. Three A sounds, all pronounced differently. Very suspicious. (Beat.) I used to have pet Australian leaf bugs in my dorm, and one was named Betty, except you couldn't tell them apart, so they were all Betty. Then stupid Kallan stepped on, like, five Bettys. Brooklyn was furious.

MATTHEW

Hmm. Right. Um, we'll talk later, and I will see you later. (Beat.) Bye now.

> Daisy shrugs and pulls out her phone. Matthew, flustered, leaves in the direction of the bookstore. Classes are done for the day and people are flocking to the plaza to socialize. In the distance, helicopters are scanning the desert for Chris and Rhys, and also, it's time for a commercial.

> * * *

> Back at Sea Breeze Academy, Brooklyn and Virgo are shelving Young Adult novels as Matthew enters the SBA

bookstore. The girls are wearing orange polos tucked into their little white shorts. Brooklyn stands when she sees Matthew. Virgo stands as well. Elsewhere, Chris and Rhys are hallucinating on peyote leaves.

BROOKLYN

Matthew!

VIRGO

Bless you.

BROOKLYN

Where have you been?! You were supposed to be here, like, a long time ago!

MATTHEW

Oh, um, sorry. I saw your cousin. (Scratching the back of his neck.) What did I miss?

VIRGO

Well, we both got the job, for starters.

MATTHEW

Hey, that's convenient, considering all the other applicants. (Beat.) I mean, congrats!

BROOKLYN

Yeah, but then a customer got mad because we don't sing "Happy Birthday."

VIRGO

We work at a bookstore, mind you.

BROOKLYN

A girl asked if we had any books by Sherlock Holmes.

VIRGO

A guy asked if we had any books by Jane Eyre.

BROOKLYN

Some punk stole every thesaurus from the reference section.

VIRGO

We had no words to express our anger.

BROOKLYN

A customer peed on my shoe.

VIRGO

And all while people are saying stuff like, "Hey, uhh, I'm looking for a book."

BROOKLYN

It's a bookstore! Great start!

VIRGO

"Yeah, uhh, I don't know the title or the author, but, uhh, I think it has a blue cover."

BROOKLYN

Or better yet: "I'm looking for a Stephen King book—you know, *the scary one*."

VIRGO

And have they tried looking the book up beforehand?

BROOKLYN

Nooooo, because that'd be too easy!

VIRGO

Matthew, I swear, working customer service is like someone whacking your kneecap with a socket wrench and then telling you to run.

BROOKLYN

Which you would've known had you been here when you were supposed to! We even sent Liss out running to find you!

VIRGO

Running, Matthew! *Socket wrench!*

MATTHEW

Okay, I get it. Jeez. You could've just texted me. (Looking around.) Where do you all keep the SBA yearbooks?

BROOKLYN

Seriously?

MATTHEW

Well, no, not like, I-want-you-to-stop-talking Where-do-you-all-keep-the-SBA-yearbooks, but like, This-is-interesting-and-yet-I'm-changing-the-subject Where-do-you-all-keep-the-SBA-yearbooks. (Beat.) I just want to check something.

VIRGO

Why do you want a yearbook? You haven't even been here since November!

BROOKLYN

Oh God. You better not be looking up that kid from the protest. So help me, Matthew, if that's what you're doing—

MATTHEW

Pulov. His name was Pulov.

BROOKLYN

Forget Pulov! You cannot care about every single issue on the planet! All you're doing is being weird! Why are you so depressing? Why can't you be happy with going to such an incredible school as Sea Breeze Academy? Why are you so fixated on this?!

MATTHEW

Why don't you care that a kid was taken away and that no one's talking about it?!

VIRGO

Hey, did you know that I'm not just ambiguously brown but that I'm actually half Peruvian?

MATTHEW

Virgo, what the heck?

> Brooklyn tosses up her hands and walks over to her backpack. There, she pulls out an SBA yearbook and then stomps over and forcefully shoves the book into Matthew's chest.

BROOKLYN

There. Have a stupid yearbook. Talk to Dean Fischer about this protesting kid if you're so concerned—fine, whatever—but if you're not gonna buy anything here, then all you're doing is loitering. So leave. Virgo and I have actual work to do.

> Brooklyn storms off into the backroom. Virgo looks at Matthew, mouths a sorry to him, and then continues shelving.
>
> Matthew examines the yearbook in his hands. From the way he sighs as he touches the school's name embossed on the front cover to how he glances back at Virgo before exiting the bookstore, it is evident that both he and Brooklyn are in for a long night, and also, it's time for a commercial.

* * *

> Back at Sea Breeze Academy, Matthew lies back on his bed at his dorm room in Wright Suites. Beside him is the yearbook. Matthew gently picks it up. He runs his finger across the spine and sighs. He lays it back down.

He closes his eyes.

BROOKLYN

Knock knock.

> Matthew glances over to see Brooklyn standing by the open doorway. Brooklyn sort of waves at him before entering the room and quietly closing the door. She then steps out of her flip-flops and joins Matthew at the foot of the bed. Brooklyn's knees pop as she sits crisscrossed, facing Matthew.

BROOKLYN (cont.)

Hey.

MATTHEW

Hey.

BROOKLYN

Sorry I yelled at ya. Y'know I was stressed, is all.

MATTHEW

(Grinning.) Your accent's coming out.

BROOKLYN

(Laughing.) I'm from Oklahoma!

> Matthew laughs with her. Brooklyn smiles. Her toes brush up against the yearbook. She notices and frowns.

BROOKLYN (cont.)

Did you find what you wanted?

MATTHEW

Haven't looked yet. Kept going back and forth on whether I wanted to.

BROOKLYN

He probably transferred out or something. You know that, right?

MATTHEW

Daisy said he was a refugee student. He had nowhere to go.

BROOKLYN

Well, it is against SBA rules to use profanity. I wouldn't be surprised if he got in trouble for that.

MATTHEW

But *expelled?* Really? The crime doesn't fit the punishment.

> Brooklyn and Matthew sit in silence. Brooklyn uncrosses her legs and lies on her back at the foot of the bed, staring up at the ceiling. Matthew sits upright to watch her.

BROOKLYN

Someone stole five hundred dollars from the bookstore today.

MATTHEW

What?! You guys were robbed?!

BROOKLYN

No, it was... internal theft. Certainly doesn't look good for the new girls to have half a grand go missing during their first shift.

MATTHEW

Oh my God. That's awful. So what happened?

BROOKLYN

Well, someone had to take the fall, and Virgo needs the job more than I do. So I took the blame, even though our manager knew neither of us stole the cash. She fired me. We're lucky she didn't get Dean Fischer involved. (Sighing.) I spent an hour just crying on some bench in Mintz Plaza. Then Coach Poole walked by, stopped, and asked what was wrong. I told him. And then he went into the bookstore and wrote them a check for five hundred. He wanted to clear my name. He said I have a good reputation here.

MATTHEW

Wow. That's... awesome of Coach to do.

BROOKLYN

Yeah. Yeah, it was.

> Matthew watches Brooklyn. She's crying. She shakes her head and wipes the tears away.

MATTHEW

Did you get your job back?

BROOKLYN

Huh? Oh, no, I was too... humiliated, I guess? The whole ordeal was just so messed up. And you and I had that fight before that, and with the whole Pulov kid situation... (Covering her face with her hands.) God, it's so... *suckish*.

MATTHEW

We should hang out more. You and me. We could go down to the beach like we used to. Fukutsū. Something. We haven't really done anything since I came back on prom night.

BROOKLYN

You're right. I'm sorry.

MATTHEW

I'm sorry too, Brooklyn.

BROOKLYN

You can call me Rook if you want. I know you only meant it teasingly back then. I just said that the other day because... well, because...

Brooklyn sits up and takes the yearbook.

BROOKLYN (cont.)

You want to look at this thing?

Matthew laughs. Brooklyn smiles.

MATTHEW

You do the honors. It's your yearbook.

Brooklyn carefully feels the top corners of the book. Matthew moves over beside her. Their legs touch. With a deep breath, Brooklyn opens the yearbook to a page in the middle.

Matthew frowns. Brooklyn turns to another page. Then another, and again. Brooklyn quickly flips through the entire yearbook. Each page is the same.

MATTHEW (cont.)

Why are they blank? Did you, um, accidentally get a misprint?

BROOKLYN

No. (Shaking her head.) I don't know—

The door opens. Chris helps Rhys ease his way into the room. Rhys grimaces with each step. He is noticeably red.

CHRIS

Hey, Matthew. Hey, Brooklyn.

Rhys falls back onto the bottom bunk, then cries out in pain. Chris stretches.

CHRIS (cont.)

He basically got sunburned in less than an hour.

RHYS

Like, cool, sun! Nice to see you too! God, my shoulders burn. (To Chris.) Why didn't you get burned? I put on the same stuff as you!

CHRIS

Dude, I'm black. And no, you didn't! You put on tanning oil—and don't you dare deny it, 'cause I saw you do it! (To Brooklyn and Matthew.) And hey, did you guys know the largest bloodflower cactus ever recorded became bipedal and could move its position? No one's seen it in over a decade. Crazy stuff out there, man. (Eyeing the yearbook.) Whatcha got there?

Brooklyn sits on the yearbook.

BROOKLYN

Oh, nothing. (Voice shaking.) Just a... sketchbook. So were you able to come up with thirty cactus facts?

CHRIS

Yeah, I did! I even started writing the report on my phone. Wanna hear?

Brooklyn nods, smiling. Matthew notices a single tear still caught in her eye. Chris pulls out his phone.

CHRIS (cont.)

(Clearing his throat, grinning.) Ahem. "Most species of cacti are not native to North America, but were brought over by Christopher Columbus, along with terminal illness. The cactus uses many adaptations to survive the dry heat. One example is by sweating..."

Brooklyn continues to smile while Chris reads from his phone. Rhys moans and covers his head with a pillow. Matthew glances over at Brooklyn. She's looking at him with sullen eyes. Matthew takes her hand, and she holds it close.

A bird's eye view of Sea Breeze Academy at night, and then the credits roll.

1. Hey Arthur, we're gonna open up the bypass, make sure it doesn't start to climb up or anything.
2. mumble mumble mumble
1. What's that?
2. mumble mumble mumble mumble
1. Hey bud I can't hear you.

"SURPRISE PARTY"

The gang surprises Chris for his birthday with a private concert by his favorite pop singer. Meanwhile, Virgo hunts down the food thief at the school bookstore. Guest starring Lita Candyce.

Another perfect day in Southern California. Brooklyn, Liss, Rhys, and Matthew stroll along the sidewalk under the shade of oak trees. Liss and Rhys hold hands as they walk together, with Brooklyn beside them. Matthew lags a step behind.

RHYS
Okay, okay, let me try again!

Brooklyn and Liss laugh as Rhys takes a deep breath.

RHYS (cont.)
Salty sleep snails—nope. Salty sea snapes—gaah. Salty sea snails sweeming—bleh, all right, my tang is toungled. I can't do it.

LISS
(Laughing.) You try, Brooklyn. How many times can you say, "Salty sea snails swimming slowly"?

BROOKLYN

At least once. (Beat.) Okay, not even once. I end up saying "swimming," like, four times.

LISS

And you, Matthew?

MATTHEW

Hey, Brooklyn, can we, uh, talk?

BROOKLYN

Umm, yeah, sure? What do you want to talk about?

RHYS

Salty snee sails... snotty sleep nails...

MATTHEW

I mean, like, in private? About Pulov?

> Liss looks back at Matthew, though Brooklyn keeps
> her eyes forward. Brooklyn frowns.

BROOKLYN

Just say what's on your mind, whatever it is.

MATTHEW

I... uh, Brooke, I would just really like it if we could go somewhere else for a second—

BROOKLYN

Matthew, come on, look around! It's another perfect day out. People are playing soccer, they're reading under trees, golfing, throwing Frisbees, sunning on the grass... I was late for class today because a girl convinced me to do yoga for half an hour. Where else can you do something like that? Only here, at Sea Breeze Academy. Life is great, okay? There's nothing to worry about. Life is great. Say it with me. Life is great.

Liss looks to Rhys. She smiles.

LISS

Life is great.

Rhys looks to Liss. He smiles back.

RHYS

Life is great.

MATTHEW

The yearbook—

BROOKLYN

Life is great.

LISS

Life is great.

RHYS

Life is great, dude.

MATTHEW

Life… is great.

BROOKLYN

Nothing to worry about.

LISS

Except maybe Chris's surprise party. Didn't you want to plan something, Brooklyn?

BROOKLYN

Oh, that's right! So much has gone on, I forgot it's tomorrow!

RHYS

Speaking of the birthday boy.

> The gang stops as Chris limps over with a hand against his left eye. He is accompanied by Tina, who is too short to adequately support him.

BROOKLYN

Hey, Tina! Hey… Chris? Are you okay?

> Chris squints out of his right eye.

CHRIS

Hi, ladies. Roommates. Matthew, you remember Tiny Tina, right?

MATTHEW

Your girlfriend, yeah. (Waving.) Hey, Tina.

TINA

Hey, Matthew.

> Tina smiles at Matthew, then quickly frowns as Chris groans in pain, a hand still over his eye.

TINA (cont.)

I was making him a cake—

CHRIS

(Crying in pain.) She's so swee-ee-eet!

TINA

—and he wasn't supposed to know, but then he showed up to the Dutton lounge early, and since he was there, he wanted to help.

> Chris is sobbing. Brooklyn and Liss look concerned. Matthew blinks, then glances elsewhere.

TINA (cont.)

He got this, uhh… this white stuff in his eyes.

> Rhys sneers.

RHYS

What kind of white stuff?

CHRIS

I had a butter knife of frosting, and I somehow whipped it, and it hit my eye and… and oh my God, the sugar.

BROOKLYN

Did you flush it out with water?!

CHRIS

Yeah, but I washed my hands first, and so I had soap on them and rubbed my eye and now I am *dying*.

MATTHEW

Oh gosh. That happened to me once last year with Brooklyn when I had spicy tuna for lunch and then started rubbing my eyes after. (Placing a hand on Chris's shoulder.) I feel your suffering.

LISS

Think of how the tuna suffered.

MATTHEW

Well, the tuna fulfilled its tasty purpose.

BROOKLYN

(Smiling.) There's the Matthew I know.

CHRIS

Man, can't you see I'm in pain? Partially-blind guy here, remember? Feels like death itself is licking my eyeball!

BROOKLYN

Have you been to the nurse yet?

TINA

That's where I'm trying to get him to go.

CHRIS

No way. You know I don't trust nurses.

MATTHEW

Isn't your mom a vet in Atlanta?

CHRIS

Exactly! Never cries when she has to put a pet down—it's like she's numb to it. Wildly calm. And she's always questioning every little thing I say! (Shaking his head.) I love that woman, but man, is she scary sometimes. And Nurse Morgan is ten times worse!

TINA

Come on, Chris. Let's go. The health center ought to have eye drops or something.

CHRIS

But I don't wannaaaaa...!

> Tina pulls Chris along by the hand as she walks away. Chris continues to fuss while the gang watches. Brooklyn shakes her head.

BROOKLYN

Poor Chris. We have got to throw him an awesome surprise party tonight. He won't be expecting it!

LISS

Agreed. Big guy deserves one after all that.

RHYS

Salty snails sneeze swimmingly—

>   Liss punches Rhys in the shoulder. Rhys throws up his
> hands in frustration.
>   From behind the gang comes Virgo. She wears little
> white shorts and an orange polo tucked into them. Her
> hair is loosely tied. She is visibly exhausted.

BROOKLYN

Hey, roomie. Rough day at the bookstore?

>   Virgo falls onto the grass and lies there sideways. She
> runs a hand through the front of her hair.

VIRGO

Where to begin? It was so hot and overcrowded and understaffed, and
we kept having to phone maintenance to deal with the thermostats not
working—and then some tweens threw up in the manga section, and
you'll never guess who had to clean that up—

>   Virgo points at herself with her thumbs.

VIRGO (cont.)

—and to top it all off, there's a fridge raider at work. As if there wasn't
enough drama at this school already!

RHYS

What's a fridge raider?

BROOKLYN

It's you when Chris complains you've been eating his food in your dorm's mini fridge.

RHYS

Yeah, but I bought them that fridge. It's way bigger than the standard ones we get. Plus it's got a touchscreen.

Matthew shrugs.

MATTHEW

It is a cool fridge.

VIRGO

Every day, there are passive-aggressive comments like, "Someone took my yogurt!" and "Who ate my hummus?" and "Somebody sure owes me some guac." And for the yogurt person, it's not really fair, considering the person who owned it can't eat dairy and has to resort to the expensive alternative.

LISS

That's awful! Ugh. You know how I give my rats yogurt every night, right? And it's the highlight of their day? Well, yesterday, I realized we were out of yogurt, and just when I was about to break the news to them, I decided to try mixing sour cream and strawberry coffee flavoring. And it worked! And I was surprised, because rats are generally picky eaters. Granted, I can tell Lewis and Wistar didn't like it as much, but hey, it's better than nothing.

They stare at her.

RHYS

That's... right, babe. You tried and that's what matters. (Beat.) Even if that is really, really gross.

VIRGO

Anyway... the food thing didn't bother me until my very precious chocolate mousse went missing.

BROOKLYN

(Faux gasp.) No, not the mousse!

VIRGO

Exactly! So how do I catch the fridge raider and get the justice we deserve?

RHYS

Trap it with a paper towel and put it outside to chill.

VIRGO

This is a person, Rhys, not a spider.

He crosses his arms and looks away.

RHYS

You don't know that.

BROOKLYN

So there's Chris's surprise party to plan and Virgo's food thief to catch. We could split up—

MATTHEW

I call the bookstore.

Brooklyn stares at him.

MATTHEW (cont.)

I want to, uhh, check out the yearbooks.

BROOKLYN

Okay, fine, you can go with Virgo.

RHYS

Me too. Food thief's going down.

BROOKLYN

All right, then Liss, you're with me. We'll figure out Chris's party and keep in touch with Tina to know when he'll be back. You guys'll be at the bookstore.

LISS

Keep your phones on, people!

RHYS

(Scoffing.) Why would we not?

The gang splits up, with Brooklyn and Liss continuing on to Dutton Suites while Virgo, Rhys, and Matthew turn back for the SBA bookstore, and also, it's time for a commercial.

* * *

Back at Sea Breeze Academy, Virgo, Rhys, and Matthew walk through the SBA bookstore. Virgo, now wearing a hijab around her head, waves to the cashier as they pass. At the back of the store is a door with a keypad. Virgo types in the code and then holds the door open for the boys. Meanwhile, in the girls' lounge at Dutton Suites, Brooklyn and Liss struggle to come up with a big idea for Chris's surprise party.

Inside the breakroom are a couple of plastic tables pushed together, some chairs, boxes, a trashcan, a sink, and the fridge in question. Rhys and Matthew walk up to it. Virgo shuts the door.

MATTHEW

I saw security cameras in the store, but none in here.

VIRGO

Yeah, there aren't any in the breakroom. For our privacy.

MATTHEW

It's still inside the building. If anything bad happens, the school's still liable.

RHYS

Yeah, but that'd be too easy if there was footage of the thief.

MATTHEW

Clearly.

Rhys opens the fridge and starts rummaging around inside. Virgo leans forward, her hands on one of the tables. Matthew opens a cardboard box and slowly takes out various batteries, switches, and timers, all wired up together.

RHYS

The answer is obviously laxatives.

VIRGO

No way. Besides, if I do anything too drastic, then I'll be the one in trouble.

Matthew looks up.

MATTHEW

Well, hold on. So I know you can be charged with a crime for putting laxatives in another person's food, because it's considered poisoning, but if you put it in your *own* food? And they take it? I don't think you could get in trouble. I mean, I imagine if it's for personal use—and plenty of people do use laxatives—then it should be okay since it's *your* food, and what you put in it is nobody's business. (Beat.) Unless they steal it.

VIRGO

Yeah, but when we catch the guy and confront him or whatever, I don't want that to be part of the narrative—like, *oh, what are you doing, eating my laxative-laced chocolate mousse?*

Rhys stands up, a tub of yogurt in his hand and a spoon in the other. Written on the tub in permanent marker:

"SIDDIQ'S—DO NOT EAT!!!" Rhys takes a spoonful.

RHYS

I got it. The thief likes hummus, right? We find some hummus and put small, chewable pieces of a ridiculously hot dried pepper on it. And by ridiculously hot, I mean the sort where barely anyone can bear the heat, but also with barely any scent so that they're not suspicious. No one can say you can't put peppers on your food.

MATTHEW

That sounds evil, man.

> Rhys wipes the strawberry yogurt off his cheek with the back of his hand. He then shrugs, flashing a cocky, lizard-like grin.

RHYS

What can I say? It's what I do.

MATTHEW

But can't people have really bad reactions to hot stuff? Internally?

> Rhys tosses the empty yogurt tub into the trashcan, then drops the spoon in the sink. He reaches into the fridge and pulls out a container of guacamole. Virgo glares him down. Rhys puts it back.

VIRGO

It is evil, I agree, but it'd be so easy to catch the culprit that way. They'll totally freak when they taste the pepper. Like, I don't want to shame anyone, but everyone's so fed up with it at this point.

RHYS

I dunno, man. I wouldn't spare anybody who takes my mousse.

MATTHEW

You do know we're talking about the dessert and not the hair-styling foam, right?

RHYS

Uhh... yes!

VIRGO

Okay, so it's settled. We'll get some hummus, sprinkle some Carolina Reaper on it, put it in the fridge, and then wait for the culprit. We'll catch them red-handed—erm, red in the face!

MATTHEW

This plan has a lot of assumptions built into it.

VIRGO

Oh, stop your whining. You worked in the cafeteria last year, right? You think you can snag us some hummus?

RHYS

And I'll order in the Reaper with my one-hour delivery perk.

> Rhys waves his mother's platinum credit card. Matthew frowns.

MATTHEW

So let's get this straight. You want me to *steal* some hummus from the caf? We're going to become thieves to catch one?

RHYS

He has a point.

MATTHEW

Finally! Thank you!

RHYS

How do we know there's only one food thief?

MATTHEW

No! That's not what I meant!

VIRGO

True. It might be more than one thief. But then when the first thief goes down, it could be a sort of message, like, *I know what you guys are doing.*

MATTHEW

Why don't you just bring this up with your managers? (Crossing his arms.) Or do they only care when it's money gone missing?

VIRGO

Oh, they're aware, but nothing's being done on account of them not knowing who it is.

Matthew opens a different box. Standard yearbooks with standard covers, but the pages are all blank. He examines the box and runs a finger across the return label to Quality Copy, Ltd. in Los Angeles.

MATTHEW

This doesn't seem right. I don't know about—

Rhys's phone vibrates audibly from his pocket. He pulls it out, then puts it up to his ear.

RHYS

Yo, babe, what's up? Figure out what to do for Chris yet?

Matthew walks over to one of the other doors in the room and tries it. It's locked. He tries another, also locked. On the floor is a lightbulb catalog. Rhys is still talking into his phone.

RHYS (cont.)

Lita Candyce? The pop singer? She was at one of my mom's yacht parties… yeah, I'm sure we could arrange something. I'll text my mom and let you know.

Rhys puts his phone away.

RHYS (cont.)

That was Liss and Brooklyn. They want to see if I can get Lita Candyce to come sing "Happy Birthday" to Chris.

VIRGO

Hey, that's a great idea! He loves her stuff. You take care of that, and Matthew will steal some hummus from the caf. I'll stay here and look pretty. We'll meet back in an hour.

Virgo claps her hands.

VIRGO (cont.)

Let's boogie!

MATTHEW

This is... weird.

RHYS

Boogie, Matthew! Be a sport!

Virgo gestures toward the door. Matthew opens his mouth to protest, then sighs with defeat. He exits.

In the bookstore is the cashier behind the register. She is scrolling through her phone. Only her right thumb moves. Matthew walks past her on his way outside.

Matthew walks down the steps and turns left for Mintz Plaza. There, the same two kids as always are tossing a Frisbee to each other while some others sit on nearby benches as they text. Matthew recognizes a few girls in shorts and bikini tops standing by the entrance to Fukutsū, but they don't seem to be speaking—they just sort of move their lips and then roll their heads back as they mime laughing at an imaginary anecdote.

The palm trees sway gently as a drone flies overhead.

Matthew walks faster.

He bypasses the cafeteria for the health center. There, through an open window, he sees Chris, Tina, and crazy Nurse Morgan, in her orange scrubs, running around the infirmary. Matthew learns from listening in that the big, angry nurse is convinced Chris has heartburn, but Chris says he does not, citing his eye as the cause of his pain. Nurse Morgan, incompetent as ever, says Chris needs a cure for his heartburn and is forcing a cup of pickle juice on him. They scream about this for ten minutes, shouting variations of "I don't have heartburn!" and "Drink the pickle juice!" with wild gesticulation. Tina tries to separate the two. Nothing is resolved.

At Wright Suites, Matthew heads up to his dorm room and opens the fridge. Sure enough, there's hummus inside, and on top of the container, a sticky note with Chris's name.

Matthew takes the hummus, then walks over to his bed. He lies back. He feels bad for Chris and Chris's eye and the whole pickle juice fiasco. He's not sure when things first got weird, but then again, he hasn't had this much time to be alone with his thoughts. He's so busy—always doing something with somebody, it seems. What even are his thoughts?

He thinks it would be ideal to live life as an oyster. Specifically, a farmed oyster. He could sit all day and filter feed. Maybe make a pearl if he wanted. But then he wouldn't be using his natural talents.

Matthew rolls over to look at the clock. Twenty

more minutes before he has to meet up again with Rhys and Virgo. He closes his eyes, pondering what life inside a shell would be like, and also, it's time for a commercial.

* * *

Back at Sea Breeze Academy, Virgo opens the door to the breakroom to let Matthew back inside. Behind him is Rhys with a package labeled "One Carolina Reaper—caution: hot!" Meanwhile, Brooklyn and Liss sneak teen pop sensation Lita Candyce out from her limo and onto campus.

Rhys sets the package on one of the tables. Virgo stares at the floor and shakes her head slowly.

VIRGO

I keep thinking about my chocolate mousse. No one deserves what I went through.

Virgo looks up.

VIRGO (cont.)

Remember how I said we should sprinkle a tiny helping of pepper on the hummus? Yeah, no. We're gonna give them the spice of a lifetime. We're going to use every last atom of pepper in our possession to catch them. And absolutely no milk.

RHYS

I got the pepper.

MATTHEW

Yeah, and, uh, I got the hummus.

> Matthew sets the hummus beside the package. The sticky note is still attached.

VIRGO

Now time to blend it all up.

MATTHEW

Like, in a blender.

RHYS

Has to be enough that no one would be able to handle the kick.

VIRGO

I'll leave the food prep to you boys. I'll set the trap.

> Matthew watches as Virgo empties the box of yearbooks. She then holds the box upright with a forked stick and ties a piece of rope to the stick.
>
> Matthew looks back. The hummus has a generous helping of Carolina Reaper evenly mixed throughout. Rhys holds it high, Virgo applauds, and then Rhys gets down on his hands and knees as he carefully places the desirable food beneath the box.
>
> Rhys stands and wipes the sweat from his brow. He gives the two a thumbs-up. Virgo then takes the end of the rope and rushes underneath the tables. Rhys hops down and joins her below.

MATTHEW

What.

VIRGO & RHYS

Shhh!

MATTHEW

Don't shush me!

VIRGO & RHYS

Shhhhh!

MATTHEW

I've been shushed.

> Matthew scratches his head, then crouches down to look at them.

MATTHEW (cont.)

How would this possibly work?

RHYS

Dude. Come on. When the thief tries to steal the food, we pull on the rope, the stick collapses, and the thief is trapped. Even I understand this.

MATTHEW

Why wouldn't you just put the hummus in the fridge—you know, where the thief expects it to be?

Matthew opens the fridge. Inside is the same container of guacamole, now empty, this time with a note attached. Virgo and Rhys get up from under the tables. Matthew holds the note out for them to read. *Myself understand to what you are trying to planned*, it says. *Better luck next anytime, you freakish goobers!*

VIRGO

That's just rude. (Beat.) And a bit, well, patronizing.

RHYS

Our plan would have worked.

MATTHEW

No, it wouldn't have! Gaah, this is… messed up! Why are you both acting so strange?! What happened to Pulov?! Why are the yearbooks completely empty?! Why was that English so poor?!

RHYS

The yearbooks?

MATTHEW

And this whole little running-around-to-try-and-catch-a-food-thief bit could've all been avoided if you'd just start putting your food in a locked container. It's that simple!

VIRGO

No! This needs to be a safe campus! Students need to feel their property won't be messed with! My managers won't do anything, our teachers won't do anything, and Dean Fischer won't do anything. So it's up to us!

MATTHEW

So you did ask the dean?

VIRGO

Why would I? Adults are useless!

> One of the previously locked doors bursts open, and out runs a six-foot-tall cactus across the room and through the door leading to the bookstore. Virgo screams, and Matthew jumps back. Rhys leaps onto one of the tables, pointing.

RHYS

That's it! The bloodflower cactus—there! The cactus is the food thief!

> Rhys leaps off the table and rushes out of the breakroom. Virgo quickly follows suit, as does Matthew. The cactus pushes past racks of backpacks and shelves of yearbooks—which fall to the floor, all blank—as Rhys, Virgo, and Matthew run in pursuit.
>
> The cashier screams, throwing her hands up in shock. Her phone goes flying, and the screen shatters as it hits the floor. Rhys steps on it as the cactus escapes out the door and down the wide flight of outdoor stairs.

RHYS (cont.)

Stop! Hey, somebody stop that cactus!

MATTHEW

Where—where is it going?!

VIRGO

There, look! The condescending con's descending!

MATTHEW

Seriously, Virgo?!

> The cactus rushes through Mintz Plaza. Students scream as they move out of its way or get pushed aside.
>
> One of the ridiculously average Frisbee kids tosses the disc. The other's too busy watching the ensuing chaos. The Frisbee flies past the distracted kid and into the plaza, where it hits the cactus dead in its center with a loud thwack.
>
> The cactus stumbles over in pain, groaning as it trips and collapses into the drained fountain. Virgo, Rhys, and Matthew run over to it.

VIRGO

You... you...

> Virgo puts her hands on her knees as she struggles to catch her breath. She points at the cactus.

VIRGO (cont.)

You stole my chocolate mousse, you jerk!

MATTHEW

But it's a... it's a costume?

RHYS

I'll bet you it's Lita Candyce. She's always wearing crazy outfits.

VIRGO

Or! Or! Maybe it's Denzel Davis going undercover!

MATTHEW

Why would it be either of those two?!

RHYS

Colonel Mustard with the lead pipe in the conservatory!

> Rhys pulls the head of the cactus to reveal the thief as Miki Mizushima. The crowd gasps. Miki now has sunken, bloodshot eyes, unnaturally pale skin, a chipped-off ear, and liver spots on her neck and lower cheeks.
> Virgo steps forward.

VIRGO

Miki...? Is that... are you...?

MATTHEW

She... was your roommate.

VIRGO

But... Miki. Where's Siddiq?

The crowd parts for Siddiq, who stands in a white undershirt and blue boxer shorts, pointing at Miki in the fountain. Behind Siddiq is Dean Fischer, along with the men in suits.

DEAN FISCHER

Hey, hey, hey, what is going on here?!

VIRGO

Miki, we... thought you transferred schools. Why are you—or, why did you...?

Miki laughs. It is shrill and uncomfortable.

MIKI

Oh, is this what those tell you, huh? Bunch of goobers tell you myself having transferred outward! Is this right, Dean Fischer? Huh?! Myself transferred outward?!

The men in suits remove Miki from the former fountain. She screams and she kicks, and yet they carry her off, away from the scene and Mintz Plaza.

Dean Fischer straightens his tie.

DEAN FISCHER

Wow. Okay, um, first: sorry. About that.

Dean Fischer rubs his forehead.

DEAN FISCHER (cont.)

We'll... be taking it from here. And thank you, Virgo, Rhys... Matthew.

> Dean Fischer nods, then leaves with the remaining men. The crowd disperses.
>
> The sky is tinged with a wash of blue-orange-crimson. Virgo shivers. She scratches her left hand with the right.

VIRGO

We should get to Chris's party.

RHYS

Yeah. You're right.

> Rhys bends down to pick up the Frisbee. He tests it in his hand, sighs, and then hurls it off into the distance. He exits.
>
> Virgo starts walking away, but Matthew grabs her arm.

VIRGO

What are you—?

MATTHEW

What's going on, Virgo?

VIRGO

Matthew—

Matthew squeezes her arm tighter, a low-burning anger inside him. Virgo cries out in pain.

MATTHEW

What is happening here?! Stop talking around it!

VIRGO

Matthew, God, you're hurting me!

MATTHEW

Why won't you answer me?!

Virgo slumps to the ground in tears. Matthew lets go of her arm. She cries into her hands. Matthew curses under his breath.

MATTHEW (cont.)

This is ridiculous. I'm leaving—

VIRGO

No! Don't!

Virgo grabs his hand. Matthew tries to get her off, but she holds him tight.

MATTHEW

Cut it out! Cut it all out!

VIRGO

No, no no no, please, Matthew, I need you! I need you right now—

right now, with you, is what I need. None of this craziness.

MATTHEW

So you admit this is crazy?!

VIRGO

Yes, of course, yes, this is all so... (Between short sucks of air.) Yes. Please. I will explain everything to you—alone, later. When we're alone, I will, I promise. We just have to get through this. Right now. Please, Matthew, behave. For me. For Brooklyn. Pretend things are how they were. Pretend this is normal. Please.

MATTHEW

Fine! Fine. Whatever.

VIRGO

I'm sorry. But thank you.

MATTHEW

Whatever.

> Matthew looks at Virgo, then eases his way down next to her. She lets go of his hand. They watch the sun sinking into the horizon like this.

VIRGO

I told you, the other day, that I'm Peruvian. Well, in the last week, there's been a lot of natural disasters there. Landslides. Flooding. It's affected mostly areas near rivers and hills, so my family's been spared from that, thankfully, but... the water supply has been cut. And water bottles are too expensive, and sold out, and... I'm just really worried about some of my friends and family who live in the affected areas, and one of them lost her house, and I feel so... powerless? Helpless?

> Virgo wipes the tears from her eyes. She sniffs.

VIRGO (cont.)

I wish I could stop all this. And I'm so annoyed because here we're so used to having almost everything, when down there, my family is forced to use plastic utensils so they don't have to wash anything... and yet I can't stop finding things to complain about here. We're supposed to be all upbeat and cheery. You think too much. I think too much. And we should be grateful, you know? Life is great at SBA.

MATTHEW

Yeah. I've heard that before.

VIRGO

I just hope this passes soon. All of it.

> They sit in a cold, eerie silence. Matthew expects to see some seagulls flying around, but there are only dark storm clouds up ahead, long and layered. The wind rattles the palm trees and churns the waves down below, and for a moment, he thinks he hears Lita Candyce singing "Easy Dreams" for Chris, Liss, Rhys, and Brooklyn. The song's simplistic chord progressions carry over the campus, tucked away in the rolling hills, and also, it's time for a commercial.

* * *

Back at Sea Breeze Academy, Virgo and Matthew join Brooklyn, Chris, Liss, Rhys, and Tina in the girls' lounge in Dutton Suites. The room is decorated with streamers and balloons of every size and color. Electropop singer and teen idol Lita Candyce sings her hit single "Easy Dreams" on a raised stage, along with the repeated verse of "Capitalism is wonderful!" Coincidentally, she is also dressed as a cactus. Bottles of Whazz^{TM} cover the tables.

VIRGO

Happy birthday, Chris!

Rhys blows a noisemaker. Chris turns around. He's wearing dark sunglasses, a party hat, and a big and giddy grin on his face. He hugs Matthew and Virgo. Rhys pats Chris on the back.

CHRIS

Awww, thanks, you guys! Man, y'all are the best, you know that?

VIRGO

Chris, my dude, you brighten our day when you walk into the room.

LISS

You're one of the funniest, most dedicated, most spirited people we know.

BROOKLYN

You were the first to welcome me to campus, and you always made sure I knew you were there for me. You always crack me up when I'm feeling down, and you've added so much to each of our lives these past couple of years. We're—and I'm not even joking when I say this—but we're honestly so blessed to call you our friend.

RHYS

So basically, you rock, bro. Even if you do snore like a seal.

VIRGO

Matthew?

MATTHEW

Oh, uhh, yeah. He does have bad adenoids.

> The gang laughs. Matthew smiles.

RHYS

Snore... like a seal... snore like a seal. Salty sea snails swimming slowly. Hey! Salty sea snails swimming slowly!

LISS

Yay! You did it, babe!

> Rhys blows the noisemaker. All laugh once more—even Matthew this time.

BROOKLYN

So did you catch the food thief?

> Virgo puts her hand on Matthew's shoulder.

VIRGO

Ah, yes. Turns out we were the thieves all along—Matthew, Rhys, and me—for failing to realize that *friendship* is the true measure of happiness, *not* the amount of chocolate mousse in a fridge. We were the problem.

RHYS

Well, the three of us and fascism.

VIRGO

That's right. Dang fascists!

> Virgo waves a determined fist in the air. The crowd cheers. Matthew smiles incredulously.
> A quick view of the party, and then the credits roll.

1. Hello Arthur?

2. Where you at?

1. The pump house.

2. Coming.

1. Between 5-2 and 5-10.

2. OK.

SEASON 5, EPISODE 4:

"LIGHTS OUT"

A storm knocks out all power on campus.
Without their technology, the gang must cooperate to stay sane.

A nother perfect day in Southern California, apart from the lightning and pouring rain. Brooklyn, Virgo, Chris, Liss, Rhys, and Matthew sit on a couple of couches in the girls' lounge in Dutton Suites. Matthew and Brooklyn sit near each other, a pillow between them. Rhys has his arm around Liss while Virgo has her feet up on the coffee table. Virgo wears her hijab, and Chris dons a pirate's eyepatch. All face the TV and absentmindedly drink from bottles of Whazz™. No one's said anything for the past hour.

On the screen is an episode of *Animal Nannies*, starring Vicki Toyger and Trixie Maltese. The ladies are prepping for a rather intense dog bath.

VICKI TOYGER
All right. Almost ready.

> Vicki puts on two pairs of rubber gloves. Trixie looks
> at her skeptically.

VICKI (cont.)

I've heard doubling up is safer—gives extra protection. (Beat.) I think. Anyway, what about you? You're not allergic to latex, are you?

TRIXIE MALTESE

(Grinning.) Nope. *That* I know for sure.

> A wiener dog perks its head up. Cue laugh track.
>
> The lights flicker in the girls' lounge. The gang looks around. Suddenly, thunder. The TV goes out as the lights flicker once more. The lights come back up, but the TV does not.

VIRGO

Awww, and that's such a great show—new episodes Thursday nights at nine, eight Central, on Channel K for Kidz, a Parrot Entertainment company.

> Virgo stands and walks over to the windows. She pulls back the curtains to reveal a darkened sky and harsh winds threatening to uproot several palms. One shivering girl struggles with her umbrella before she's knocked off her feet in a comical fashion. The lights flicker again, and this time, they're out a moment longer.

LISS

Ah rats.

RHYS

Really, babe? Again with the rats?

VIRGO

Wow. It's really storming out.

CHRIS

This is good. We need this, with the drought.

RHYS

Yeah, but what about when we need to get back to our dorm?

Rhys points to his head with both hands.

RHYS (cont.)

I *cannot* get this hair wet. (Pulling out his phone.) Here, I'll just call the news station and have the weatherman change it for us.

BROOKLYN

That's not how it works.

Rhys defiantly puts the phone up to his ear.

BROOKLYN (cont.)

No matter how much money your mom has.

Rhys lowers the phone and slouches back. Virgo returns to the couches. She smiles.

VIRGO

My grandpa used to tell me that he could make the rain stop. He would clap his hands as we drove under a bridge and go, "On" and "Off."

Virgo claps for emphasis.

VIRGO (cont.)

And so I believed with all my li'l heart that Grandpa Torres could control the weather.

BROOKLYN

(Smiling.) That's actually really sweet. Comforting.

MATTHEW

I... I don't remember... anything. From my childhood.

BROOKLYN

Anyway—

LISS

No, wait... I mean... neither can I. (Looking to Brooklyn.) Is that... weird? Oh my God. In my mind, elementary years and below are... nearly nonexistent.

CHRIS

Oh, phew, I'm not alone. When people talk to me about, like, really specific childhood memories, sometimes I'll make things up just so I don't seem crazy. To be honest, I don't remember much before, like, eleven.

VIRGO

I'd love it if I could vividly remember every moment that made me the way I am today. I'm sure it would be totally scarring, of course, but it would be worth it to know.

LISS

No, guys, this is different, this is...

Brooklyn stares at her.

LISS (cont.)

It feels like this overhanging sense of dread—

VIRGO

One that makes you want to avoid all windows at night because you swear someone or something will be out there looking back at you.

Lightning brightens the entire sky. For a moment, a humanoid figure can be seen out in the rain, watching the gang in a tense, suspicious silence. No one notices.

MATTHEW

Maybe I'm dead. Maybe I got crushed by a tree, and here I am, a ghost.

CHRIS

Obviously what you gotta do is start haunting somebody.

RHYS

Guys, I'm not getting a signal with this thing.

Rhys taps the side of his phone, holds it high in the air, and then checks the screen. He frowns.

RHYS (cont.)

No WiFi, no nothin'.

>All but Rhys take out their own phones to try. Rhys
>shakes his head.

RHYS (cont.)

Really, dudes? I have the nicest phone out of all of you. If my TSC Dreamscape GX Prime S Plus Close-Parenthesis™ can't handle the storm, neither will yours.

CHRIS

Must be the apocalypse out there then. TSC® smartphones can get service anytime, anywhere!

MATTHEW

Uhh, guys, maybe we should get back to our dorm before it gets any worse.

VIRGO

Or you could wait it out?

RHYS

No way. Nope, nope, nopeddy nope-nope. I can always fix my hair again, but no phone—no WiFi—I, no, I cannot, *cannot* do this. Nope. I need my Internet. Come on, fellas. I have my own setup back at the room. We'll use it to get the WiFi back up—to call for help or something.

>The lights flicker, then go out for good this time. The
>gang stands as thunder booms and rocks the lounge.
>Brooklyn, Virgo, Chris, and Liss scream in the dark.

LISS

Baby?! Baby, grab my arm!

RHYS

I got you!

BROOKLYN

That is *not* her arm!

MATTHEW

Dude!

RHYS

Aaack—sorry. This is nuts. We need to leave.

> By the bursts of lightning, Rhys stumbles over to the front
> doors. He pushes against them. They don't budge.

RHYS (cont.)

Huh? Oh come on! They're electric?! How is that safe?!

LISS

And of course we're in the only building without fire alarms or a
working sprinkler system.

MATTHEW

Brooklyn, where's your dorm advisor?

BROOKLYN

Sage? She and her husband were fired for embezzling.

VIRGO

We caught them last semester.

MATTHEW

So there's no adult to help us?!

VIRGO

The school's still, um, searching for their replacements—

MATTHEW

There's *nobody* here but us?!

CHRIS

And we're trapped! *We're trapped and we're all gonna di-ie-ie!*

BROOKLYN

We aren't going to die, Chris.

CHRIS

And I never told Tiny Tina that I love her! I only heavily implied it! And now... and now she'll never know because I suppressed my true feelings in case she thought I was too clingy or emotional or whatever. And... and it's all my fault.

LISS

Chris, that's...

Liss looks over to Rhys and frowns.

LISS (cont.)

I'm sure she'd love to hear you say that.

VIRGO

Aww, Chris, are you crying?

CHRIS

No, I'm not crying!

> Chris is crying. Brooklyn takes out her phone and switches on the flashlight feature.

BROOKLYN

Guys, guys. We're fine, all right? It's like that heatwave last August. We were locked inside the gym for six hours with no power, with no air conditioning or our phones—and we figured it out. We can do this!

VIRGO

Also, sorry, just wanted to say I put Special Mud™ on my face and now it's *indescribably* soft. I also shaved my legs with it. They're like vanilla-scented dolphins!

> An earsplitting crack of thunder, followed by Liss screaming at the top of her lungs.

MATTHEW

What?! What is it?!

LISS

The service tunnels! I totally forgot!

CHRIS

Gaah, my *heart!*

LISS

Oh calm down. See, there are so many stairs and narrow pathways on this campus that transporting heavy equipment is practically impossible aboveground. So the school's architects built these connecting tunnels below us to connect various buildings together—so they could haul supplies and machinery.

BROOKLYN

Is there a tunnel under Dutton Suites?

LISS

I believe so, yes!

RHYS

A tunnel? Down there? (Gulping.) Oh no. Nope, no can do, no. Ain't happening.

MATTHEW

What? This is a way out. Think about your Internet, your hair products!

CHRIS

Rhys is claustrophobic, man. He has an anxiety disorder.

VIRGO

Yeah, if he's triggered, he'll have a panic attack.

BROOKLYN

We shouldn't force this onto him.

MATTHEW

I just thought—

LISS

I'll stay. The tunnels should be pretty straightforward. Well, they're curved, but you get what I mean. Besides, I should make sure Lewis and Wistar are okay.

RHYS

You're sticking around for the rats?!

LISS

And for you, of course, my... my adorable Romeo cuddle... bunny!

> Rhys turns away, arms crossed.

RHYS

Forget it.

BROOKLYN

It's a good idea, Liss. You stay behind with Rhys, and we'll go looking for help. Matthew, you guide the way.

MATTHEW

You want me to lead?

BROOKLYN

Yes, you, in the front. Now go!

> Matthew leans over to kiss or hug or even to touch Brooklyn. She deflects. The rain pours faster, sharper.

CHRIS

Don't worry, Rhys. We got this. For our school, for WiFi, and for Tiny Tina.

LISS

And a way out of this.

> Brooklyn, Virgo, Chris, and Matthew use the flashlights on their phones to step around the furniture and over to the faint exit sign in the far corner. Matthew gives a final, goofy wave to Rhys and Liss, and the dramatic music starts to swell when they don't reciprocate.
>
> Lightning, followed by an ungodly, unworldly sound. The outside figure drags away the same umbrella girl as before, and also, it's time for a commercial.

* * *

> Back at Sea Breeze Academy, Brooklyn, Virgo, Chris, and Matthew inch their way by the light of their phones through the old and dusty SBA service tunnels, which are decaying in filth and animal droppings. Suddenly, Chris's phone dies, followed next by Virgo's, then Brooklyn's. Matthew checks his battery life. Ten percent. Meanwhile,

Liss and Rhys attempt to define their relationship as the downpour continues.

VIRGO

Well, crap, that's not good.

MATTHEW

Are we allowed to say "crap" now?

VIRGO

What? I don't know.

They walk. Overhead, the sound of thunder grows louder.

BROOKLYN

Does anyone have a legitimate flashlight?

CHRIS

Nah, I let Rhys bum mine.

VIRGO

Your flashlight?

CHRIS

Oh, *flashlight*. Uhhh, no. No lantern, torch, or beacon here.

MATTHEW

It's fine, guys. We just... have to be brave. Like Captain Canary.

CHRIS

You know he only wears that mask just so the mayor doesn't know who to bill for all the stuff he blows up while saving the day.

MATTHEW

That is a dirty lie!

Something shuffles up ahead.

VIRGO

Oh my God, was that a rat?!

BROOKLYN

No, no, I—I think that was a mouse?!

VIRGO

Well, what's the difference?!

MATTHEW

Liss would know.

BROOKLYN

Matthew, give me the phone!

Matthew hesitates. Brooklyn takes the phone, shines it around, and then walks faster. Virgo, Chris, and Matthew follow.

VIRGO

Um, I think we're good, 'cause mice live outside and rats live inside.

(Beat.) Or was it that they're six-dimensional?

BROOKLYN

Chris, you're in biology.

CHRIS

I'm pretty sure a rat has a skeleton and mice do not.

VIRGO

That's ridiculous. If it eats cheese, it's a mouse. If it doesn't, it's a rat.

CHRIS

Why would mice eat cheese if they don't have skeletons? They don't need the calcium!

> Miki jumps out in front of them, her grin wide and deranged and twitching. Brooklyn, Virgo, Chris, and Matthew scream in surprise. Virgo jumps into Chris's arms—he drops her. Embarrassed, he helps her to her feet. Miki's skin is a chalk white, her veins are visibly black, and dark circles draw attention to her wild, bloody eyes and hollow cheeks. Brooklyn tilts her head quizzically.

BROOKLYN

Miki...? Are you Miki?

> Miki nods, still grinning.

VIRGO

We, uhh, Brooklyn, um, we saw her—me, Matthew, and Rhys saw her—the other night. She was running, through campus, in a… cactus costume. (Beat.) Siddiq was in his underwear.

CHRIS

His underwear? Really?

> All look over at Chris, who pulls up his eyepatch, rubs his eyes, blinks twice, and then lowers the patch.

MATTHEW

We thought she was the food thief.

BROOKLYN

The… food thief.

> Brooklyn looks from Matthew to Virgo to Miki.

BROOKLYN (cont.)

Miki… we were told you left for a school in Australia. (Shaking her head.) We made you that card with the kangaroo on the front that said, "Get Good Learnin." And… have you… have you been down here this whole time?

> Miki howls with laughter.

MIKI

Down here?! Down under?! Ohhh, you are a poor, innocent, blonde little goober, you are. To what happen to you four? Myself listened.

Everyone here the sound same! This means, on an effort in the department of redundancy department to will away the taking earlier problem for stereotypical characters, those every become bland! Bland goobers! While you all enjoy this California coastline, sunny days, and easy life, myself survive on *canned beans and watered fountain!*

CHRIS

(Leaning in to whisper.) What's going on?

MIKI

Brooklyn, Brooklyn. Matthew, yours boyfriend, himself tells you, himself knows. Myself listened, remembered? Our everyone understand you are only that little toothpick in that tube top. Little Missed Perfect!

> Brooklyn turns to face Matthew, inadvertently shining the light in his eyes.

BROOKLYN

What is she saying? What is she talking about?!

MATTHEW

I don't know!

MIKI

Not "stereotypes," says dean ex machina. Those're "classic" types! Please. To conditionally the to! The kids are all thin, whiteness, and gorgeous, taking token minorities, or the fat kid to play the freakish outcast. This quasi-feminist crusader—to everyone around, shopping, short skirts, and lip gloss. Brooklyn is beautiful, popularity, athletic, creative, everyone goes to the girl for advice. Herself perfect? Not perfect! No, no, no!

> Miki walks up to Matthew. With her back hunched, they are exactly the same height. She grins once more, her eyes trickling blood.

MIKI (cont.)

Myself understand you understand. When have you first noticed things was weird?

MATTHEW

Ummm, this is pretty weird right now.

> Miki stomps hard on Matthew's foot. He brings it to his chest in pain, hopping on one foot. Brooklyn shines the light down in alarm, revealing Miki's feet as being three-toed and clawed.

MIKI

You believe me, myself understand this. It is the only thing you are believe to be true. Convey, Matthew. Convey them! Convey them to what you are achieved trying to said: when have you first noticed things was weird? First! When?!

MATTHEW

The Pulov kid.

BROOKLYN

No, please, not this again—

Virgo puts her hand on Brooklyn's shoulder.

VIRGO

Just let him, Brooke.

Brooklyn shrugs her off, then shoots Matthew a sideways look.

BROOKLYN

What is wrong with you?

MATTHEW

Nothing!

BROOKLYN

This isn't funny, Matthew.

MATTHEW

I'm not trying to be funny!

BROOKLYN

Well then, be funny! Don't be so... this! Just cut it out—or someone else will, and you really, really don't want that to happen.

Miki rubs the front of her face in exasperation.

MIKI

Video child... you will die, Matthew. She will convince you to do, dreaming wide awake. Myself would do helped everyone understood. Myself'll shown you are what these freakish goobers in need of will to us to do. Myself'll shown you the man with a box over his head.

> Miki faces forward and walks ahead a few steps. Matthew, Virgo, Chris, and Brooklyn join her. Miki stops, looks over her shoulder at Matthew.

MIKI (cont.)

Where was you are lasted semester?

MATTHEW

Alaska.

MIKI

To what is Alaska to you?

MATTHEW

Cold.

MIKI

Vast, bleak, unforgiving terrain. Not peppered with palm trees. Lamena. *Rebirth*. Oh, how the snow mutes the world.

> Up ahead is a door, marked only by age and neglect. Miki opens it—emitting a grinding, stuttered sound—and then slowly walks through. They follow.
>
> The gang ascends a flight of stairs to find themselves outside Dean Fischer's office in the administration building. The power is still out. Through the windows, they see it is now nighttime, and the storm continues its rage in the smothering darkness.

There's a clean light coming from under the door to Conference Room 101. Miki steps in front of it, then puts her open hand out behind her so that the others stop. She places her head against the wall, listening. Matthew, Virgo, Chris, and Brooklyn do so as well.

Matthew hears several voices, speaking low and inarticulately. They sound professional. Matthew recognizes one of the men as Dean Fischer.

DEAN FISCHER

… but giving him an eyepatch—that's a development…

WOMAN

… and this thing, with her and the rats, it needs to stop…

HOARSE MAN

… with Mike and Arthur at the pumping station…

SOFT-SPOKEN MAN

… losing control, you know. They've already started pulling plugs from upstairs…

HOARSE MAN

… Whazz is out, and so is Blazer…

WOMAN

… the TSC sponsorship is a big deal, but it won't be enough to carry the school…

DEAN FISCHER

... at least *Animal Nannies* will owe us one, right? What they should do is...

HOARSE MAN

... *Animal Nannies*? Ha. Got a message from their staff. Not amused. Sent us leftover donkeys, and all those managed to do was fall into the empty pits from the Halloween special...

DEAN FISCHER

... assholes...

WOMAN

... Standards and Practices would never approve...

SOFT-SPOKEN MAN

... you're right, you're right...

HOARSE MAN

... did you hear about the *Scooby-Doo* reboot though? Looking for teen actors. Worst-case scenario...

DEAN FISCHER

... what about a talking dog? Could we get a talking dog? Maybe a mascot...

HOARSE MAN

... with all due respect, Charles, you don't get a say in how we proceed...

SOFT-SPOKEN MAN

… you're here as a formality…

DEAN FISCHER

… just want what's best for these kids…

WOMAN

… what in the world were you thinking, basing business on an *office dispute* just to lead up to a lame pun at the end?! "Condescending con descending"—no! So someone eats your lunch, ooohh, big deal—but that's no groundwork for…

SOFT-SPOKEN MAN

… unsurprisingly poorly received…

WOMAN

… not to mention that F-bomb…

HOARSE MAN

… family values…

SOFT-SPOKEN MAN

… hands were tied…

WOMAN

… and the freckled kid! He's fired up, causing problems…

SOFT-SPOKEN MAN

… causing problems, rallying, like he did before…

HOARSE MAN

… put him on a bus, then you brought him back for Brooklyn, and now look at the drama…

SOFT-SPOKEN MAN

… Kallan…

WOMAN

… not good drama, not our drama…

SOFT-SPOKEN MAN

… causing problems…

DEAN FISCHER

… so I'll talk to him. He's a good kid…

SOFT-SPOKEN MAN

… causing problems…

WOMAN

… look here! *Hollywood's Highest,* homepage! "Every second is filler." Who do they think…

DEAN FISCHER

… which is why we go with *VERTEX* magazine instead…

WOMAN

… a Parrot Entertainment company…

HOARSE MAN

… a family of wizards, a pop star in disguise, twin boys living in a hotel…

SOFT-SPOKEN MAN

… needs more slapstick…

HOARSE MAN

… I'll show you slapstick…

WOMAN

… what we should do is focus on our core demographic…

HOARSE MAN

… analytics? Teens in the Heartland, twelve to eighteen…

WOMAN

… bunch of farmers who can't afford TSC. Need to drop the agenda bit then. Reduce roles. Far too progressive. Their parents are hardcore right-wing Republicans, after all. Keep it SoCal, but with their redneck values and ideologies rather than what we've been…

SOFT-SPOKEN MAN

… subliminally…

WOMAN

… as if feminism can be mass-produced…

HOARSE MAN

… and we should address the critics' points head-on in guise of…

WOMAN

... paywall and merchandising...

HOARSE MAN

... subvert clichés by embracing them...

SOFT-SPOKEN MAN

... keep the main thing the main thing...

WOMAN

... can avoid erasure as the school rebrands itself...

HOARSE MAN

... corporations are people...

SOFT-SPOKEN MAN

... opinions are oppression...

HOARSE MAN

... fluffy California dream...

DEAN FISCHER

... so, what I'm hearing from you all is *no* talking dog...

WOMAN

... budget cuts, you dork! Shutting down and selling our assets! If we don't find some way to settle this mess, so help me God, I will toss you in with the donkeys myself!

Miki raises her head off the wall. Matthew, Virgo, Chris, and Brooklyn move away as well. Miki walks back to the door to the stairwell. They cautiously follow.

MIKI

Currently you are... you understand something is wrong. Phony, phony, phony. Still, time to fill. Myself'll take you to Wright Suites to have... whatever it is you are needed originate from yours room, and then yourselves'll go backward to Dutton Lounge toward Rhys and Liss. They probably broke up. Comfort her. Himself will walk away unscathed.

MATTHEW

Miki...

MIKI

No talked. It is confused, myself understand. The more strange, all the trouble, more questions than answers—myself understand. The stars are not what they seem. Now then. Fire. Walk.

There is an awkward silence, and then the teens descend the stairs to return to the tunnels. Virgo leans over to Matthew to whisper.

VIRGO

This is what I meant. The other day. When we were alone.

MATTHEW

I... figured as much.

Virgo keeps her head down. Matthew sighs. Chris repeatedly opens and closes his mouth as if he's going to say something, but he doesn't. Brooklyn, though, appears unfazed, and also, it's time for a commercial.

* * *

Back at Sea Breeze Academy, Matthew, Virgo, Chris, and Brooklyn return with whatever item they had gone to retrieve. Miki lags behind. Liss, visibly distraught, sits on one of the couches, her knees to her chin, the sky no longer storming, yet raining all the same. Absent is Rhys.

Brooklyn takes a seat beside Liss, placing an arm around her.

LISS

Is...

Liss shakes her head.

LISS (cont.)

Is true love... too hard to ask for?

BROOKLYN

No. It's just not what we expect, or even want. (Crossing her arms.) Love isn't like it is on TV.

CHRIS

What is "true love" though? Like, love is just love.

VIRGO

I believe true love is real and that we all deserve to feel it with someone, if not each other.

BROOKLYN

Thank you, Virgo. That's kind of you to say.

CHRIS

I love you guys. I hope you all know that.

VIRGO

Of course we do, big guy. That's what friends are for.

BROOKLYN

That, and hugs.

VIRGO

You know what I love most about hugs? They're inexhaustible. Everyone has a limitless number of hugs to give and receive. If anything, no one can get enough.

CHRIS

I'll hug to that!

> Brooklyn, Virgo, and Chris hug Liss. Brooklyn pulls in Matthew by the shirt, and so he places his arms around them and stiffly pats their backs. Liss smiles through the tears as the electricity comes back and the lights flick on by the true power of love, friendship, and engineering.
> Miki slow claps.

MIKI

Deep, guys! Very nice! The keeping main the thing main thing. Sooo impress.

>   Brooklyn stomps over and slaps Miki to the ground.

CHRIS

Brooklyn!

MATTHEW

Oh my God!

LISS

Miki Mizushima?!

>   Brooklyn, her blue eyes wild and furious, towers over
>   Miki, who's writhing on the floor in pain.

MIKI

Cucumbers! Basements! Skillet! Grapes!

BROOKLYN

I will pineapple-slap your ascot. I am not even joking. Go back into those tunnels and stay there. This is *not* how we do things.

MIKI

Crack in the wall! Analyst! Seaweed! Tetanus shot! Snowballs! Aaaaarghh, *something!*

Miki scrambles onto all fours and scampers off through the exit door. Brooklyn takes a deep breath.

BROOKLYN

Okay... okay... (Aiming her thumb where Miki left.) It's Scunthorpe's Syndrome. Bad words inside normal ones.

MATTHEW

Brooklyn, what did you—?!

BROOKLYN

So what did we learn today, kiddos?

VIRGO

Uhh, that, uh, that everyone seeks attention and validation in different ways.

CHRIS

That Liss is incredible just because she simply exits—*exists!*—and, um, she is loved by more people than she... probably realizes?

BROOKLYN

That we're stronger and more enduring than we think we are. We have a right to be on this earth, and we are not a waste of space at all.

VIRGO

Don't ever limit yourself, because you are full of potential.

BROOKLYN

And Liss, always stay true to yourself no matter what. Embrace who you are, including your good and bad qualities, because they are what make you, you. You're perfect the way you are—even if your rats do make you self-conscious.

VIRGO

You have so much to look forward to in life, no matter how many rough patches you have to go through.

BROOKLYN

Because, unfortunately, we all have to. But there's always going to be better days ahead, no matter what. Nothing can stay the same forever. You will get there, wherever you are going.

VIRGO

Pain is weakness leaving the body.

BROOKLYN

Your only limit is you.

> Brooklyn, with a strained smile, turns expectantly to Matthew. Virgo, Chris, and Liss follow suit.

MATTHEW

Oh, what, am I supposed to say something now? Or were you planning to *slap me in the face?!*

BROOKLYN

(Through her teeth.) Just give Liss your advice.

MATTHEW

Advice?! (Scoffing.) Advice! *To run away from this place!* To catch the next bus from here to Windhaven!

BROOKLYN

Fine then. Chris, what would *your* advice to Matthew be?

CHRIS

I'd rather not—

Brooklyn glares at Chris. He gulps.

CHRIS (cont.)

Umm... Matthew, buddy... you can be your greatest enemy, or your greatest friend.

MATTHEW

Is that a threat?! Dude!

BROOKLYN

And instead of crying, maybe try birdwatching instead. Sitting in the middle of nowhere and covering yourself in birdseed and letting the birds all land on you. Then you will know true peace.

LISS

I'm so sorry, I just—I can't do this anymore. It's too much right now.

VIRGO

Liss, don't... don't do this. Please.

Liss pushes herself off the couch and out the entrance, into the rain. Matthew watches in case she comes back, but she doesn't. The double doors swing shut.

Brooklyn saunters over to Matthew, strategically swaying her hips as she does so. She puts her hands on his shoulders. He tenses up. She slowly rubs his arms back and forth. She breathes onto his chest.

BROOKLYN

Matthew... baby... you went through a lot in Alaska. You had a busy day today. I know it's been tough on you.

MATTHEW

I don't... this is... I'm still so confused—

BROOKLYN

The focus is on me, okay? We have lots to prepare for, lots on our minds. We need to concentrate.

MATTHEW

I... I think I need an adult.

Brooklyn kisses Matthew. She presses her warm lips against his. His eyes are wide open. He looks down at her hand on his leg. He looks at her legs, tanned, smooth. She smiles, then takes a step back.

BROOKLYN

Come. Let's all just sit on the couches. We'll unwind and breathe easy. And then it'll be tomorrow before you even know it. All right?

Brooklyn stretches in a provocative way before reclining on one of the couches. Virgo lies on another. Chris opts for the floor. Matthew stares at them in disbelief.

Seconds pass. They feel like an eternity. With Brooklyn, Virgo, and Chris all sitting there with their eyes closed like that, feigning relaxation, Matthew feels as if he has no choice but to join them. So he does. He sits on the carpet with his legs crossed, and he breathes in, then out. As if he has all the time in the world.

A bird's eye view of a rainbow in the twilight descending over Sea Breeze Academy. It is peaceful. Deserved. Probably the last. And then the credits roll.

1. Got your O$_2$ analyzer. It's showing 16% right now.
2. That's low, that's bad.
1. What's 56A showing?
2. 17.7%. Still low.

"MOTHER'S DAY AT SBA"

*The mothers of SBA students are invited to campus
to spend the weekend with their children.*

A nother perfect day in Southern California. White frame tents line the edges of Jackson Commons, and grounds workers haul tables of finger foods across the green lawn and underneath the shade. In the center of the field is a raised stage with a podium and microphone. Tied to the surrounding palm trees are elegant white banners. Written in SBA orange: HAPPY MOTHER'S DAY!

A grand tourer convertible pulls up neatly beside the quad. Out walks a woman with a neat, trimmed bob and skin freshly tanned. Large bug-eyed framed sunglasses rest on her face. She glances around, then taps her foot impatiently. She pulls out her phone, the brand obscured.

RHYS
Mom! Hey!

> Rhys comes running across the big field and hugs Mrs. Underwood. She sort of pats the top of his head, sneezes lightly, and then scoots him away.

RHYS (cont.)

How are you?! How're the movies?!

MRS. UNDERWOOD

Can't talk. Non-disclosure agreements. Where are the refreshments?

RHYS

Oh, uhh, over under the tents, I think—

MRS. UNDERWOOD

Over? Under? Boy, which is it?

RHYS

Under, Mom.

MRS. UNDERWOOD

Under*wood*. Now then. Have a thousand dollars.

RHYS

Sweeeet.

A little way off, a red rental drives around in several circles before finding a parking spot next to the administration building. Mrs. Rivers steps out of the car and admires the spectacular view of the ocean and sprawling hills. Her hair has a large gray streak down the left side, and her eyes now sport crow's-feet. She touches the low-hanging leaves of a palm. She smiles.

BROOKLYN

Mom!

> Brooklyn and Daisy rush over to Mrs. Rivers. She opens her arms wide first for her daughter, then for her niece.

MRS. RIVERS

Daisy! Golly Moses, do you look older. And taller! Surpassed me by an inch or two!

> Daisy laughs.

DAISY

Thanks, Aunt Sarah. (Looking around.) Is my mom not with you?

MRS. RIVERS

Polly wanted to drive, so I'm not sure where—

> A two-door open-cab pickup suddenly lurches up the road and onto the grass in front of them. The beater's paint job is faded, the color between white and rust, suggesting decades of ownership. It also features bull horns above the hood and windshield, because Oklahoma.
>
> Inside is Aunt Polly, a large woman with tall gray hair and a belt buckle bigger than her fist. Aunt Polly exits the pickup and pours the remnants of a soda bottle out onto the grass. She tosses the bottle back inside.

AUNT POLLY

Daisy! Come 'ere to your momma, little pumpkin pie!

> Daisy hugs her mother. Brooklyn does as well. Someone lets out a tiny fart. Daisy and Brooklyn step back, Aunt Polly blushes, and Mrs. Rivers laughs. The girls laugh too.

DAISY

Ma, you have a bug in your hair.

AUNT POLLY

And you're wearing trashy makeup!

> Aunt Polly licks her thumb and tries to wipe off Daisy's eyebrow. Daisy pushes back.

DAISY

Whoa, personal space much? You think that just because you birthed me, you can get that close to me?

AUNT POLLY

And don't forget all the times I cleared your rear when you were little. So yeah, I think I have a right to get in your face. Heck, I'm pretty sure you even peed in my face!

> Rhys and Mrs. Underwood walk by.

BROOKLYN

Hey, Rhys! You remember my mom, right?

RHYS

Yeah, when she had to pick you up that one time you were homesick.

Brooklyn looks away, embarrassed. Rhys shakes Mrs. Rivers's hand.

RHYS (cont.)

And this is my mom—

Mrs. Underwood extends her hand for Mrs. Rivers.

MRS. UNDERWOOD

Mrs. Clara Underwood. Pleasure to meet you.

Aunt Polly steps in front of her sister-in-law and eagerly shakes the hand of Mrs. Underwood.

AUNT POLLY

Hi, Polly Rivers, big fan of your work, I absolutely loved you in *All the Feels*.

BROOKLYN

So your name is still "Mrs. Clara Underwood"? Even after the… well, your separation with Mr.—?

MRS. UNDERWOOD

It's registered with the Actors Guild. I couldn't change it even if I wanted.

Brooklyn looks to Rhys, who shrugs in response.

MRS. RIVERS

So, Daisy, what's new with you? Brooklyn texts and calls me all the time, but I only see you for the holidays!

DAISY

Well, I'm currently in a throuple with Fatima and Vladislav!

MRS. RIVERS

"Throuple"? What's that?

AUNT POLLY

Yeah, Daisy, you didn't tell me about no "throuple."

DAISY

Oh, it's, like, a three-way relationship. It's chill.

MRS. RIVERS & AUNT POLLY

Chill?

MRS. UNDERWOOD

That's California culture for you.

Aunt Polly crosses her arms.

AUNT POLLY

Daisy, Brooklyn, where's this dean of yours? I've been noticing things the past few years, and I wanna talk to that man about the way he's running this school.

MRS. RIVERS

It's certainly... abnormal, to say the least.

BROOKLYN

He's speaking at the luncheon today.

AUNT POLLY

Well, I sure ain't never heard a better excuse for some food.

MRS. UNDERWOOD

I wouldn't get too excited—it's mostly hot dogs and barbecue meat.

AUNT POLLY

Lead the way!

> Daisy, Mrs. Rivers, Aunt Polly, and Mrs. Underwood head in the direction of Jackson Commons. From the looks of concern Brooklyn and Rhys give each other, it's clear Dean Fischer's in for an earful later, and also, from the swell of dramatic music, that it's time for a commercial.

* * *

> Back at Sea Breeze Academy, Brooklyn, Matthew, Rhys, and a hijab-less Virgo are in line for food underneath the white tents.

VIRGO

Avocados are such a trick food. Like, here, let me be a technical fruit but a culinary vegetable that's filled with greasy fat that turns out to be healthy for you—and lemme just go ahead and look disgusting and vaguely dangerous on the outside, but also be green and fifty percent seed on the inside!

RHYS

Hey, Virgo, where's your mom?

VIRGO

Couldn't make it. Avocados *are* fruit, right?

RHYS

They have wrinkly skin, and reptiles also have wrinkly skin, so...

> Brooklyn laughs.

BROOKLYN

Come on. Our moms are waiting.

> They walk with their plates of food to one of the tables in front of the raised stage, where Daisy, Aunt Polly, Mrs. Rivers, Mrs. Underwood, Liss, Chris, and his mother— Mrs. Carmichael—are already sitting. Chris stands.

CHRIS

Hey, you guys, this is my mom, Yvonne.

BROOKLYN & VIRGO & RHYS

Hi, Mrs. Carmichael.

> Mrs. Carmichael pushes her hair twists to the side before waving at the kids. She smiles at Chris.

MRS. CARMICHAEL

So these are your friends? The ones who take you on all those adventures you're always talking about?

AUNT POLLY

Those adventures—*misadventures*, I'd call 'em. Where are the adults watching over our children, huh? What's going on here?

MRS. CARMICHAEL

Right? Look at him—you know, my son? Wearing an eyepatch? Where were the teachers then?

RHYS

Mrs. Carmichael, you're a vet, right?

MRS. CARMICHAEL

Um, that's right, Rhys, yes? Why?

RHYS

Oh, I was just wondering which war you served in and how many people you killed.

> Mrs. Underwood takes a silverware roll and whacks Rhys on the back of the head with it.

MRS. UNDERWOOD

She's a *veterinarian!* She works with animals! (Shaking her head.) You are just like your father.

> Dean Fischer steps onto the stage, where the Gay Pride flag has been replaced with the more traditional red, white, and blue. Off to the side, Denzel Davis stands with his camera crew and setup. The dean grins wide at the crowd. He motions with his hands a lot.

DEAN FISCHER

Welcome, parents and students, to Sea Breeze Academy's first eighteenth-annual Mother's Day Luncheon Program Special, broadcasting live on our *SBA News* channel. My name is Charles Fischer, the Dean of Student Affairs here. And wow, what a gorgeous Mother's Day it is!

> The crowd claps.

DEAN FISCHER (cont.)

At SBA, we believe in the instillation of self-confidence by complete child autonomy. There must be a student buy-in. Children need to feel a sense of purpose for them being at school other than the *ominous* and occasionally bleak rationale that their education is simply for them to be able to gain employment for forty-plus years after college. With the support of you, the wonderful mothers of our students, we have already accomplished so much together. We still have some ways to go, of course—they haven't graduated yet! But believe me when I say that your children are in excellent hands, and success is indeed on the horizon.

> The crowd turns left to the horizon line, where the blue of the sky meets the blue of the ocean beyond the breaking waves.
> Aunt Polly rises.

AUNT POLLY

Yeah, I have a question.

DEAN FISCHER

O-kay, that's... what's your question, Miss...?

AUNT POLLY

Polly Rivers, mother of Daisy Rivers. We're from Oklahoma, and you might say we have a bit of a rural, country way to our home life and mannerisms and farming and whatnot. Well, when my daughter came back after a semester here, she was different—all about miniskirts and makeup. And that's fine. But I'm under the impression that these SoCal trust-fund kids attempted to change my daughter's, erm, *agrarian* ways so that she could fit in more at SBA and be popular. Well? What do you say to that?

> The crowd is silent. The women fan themselves with their
> cloth napkins. Dean Fischer refers briefly to his notes.

DEAN FISCHER

Umm, so, at Sea Breeze Academy, we believe that our students need to be exposed to norms and circumstances different from the lifestyles and situations their parents permit them—if only for the children to flourish and reach proper independence—which can only be beneficial in such a safe, *productive* environment as is our campus.

AUNT POLLY

And you're teaching all that while spoiling these kids?! They've got a sushi bar, laptops everywhere—

DEAN FISCHER

Okay, which, if I may point out, are paid for with the entrance fee.

AUNT POLLY

—flat-screens in every room, stylish dorms to hang out in… and why is it my kid never seems to be in class for more than five minutes a day?

DAISY

Mom!

        Mrs. Rivers stands.

MRS. RIVERS

Hi, Sarah Rivers here, mother to Brooklyn, aunt to Daisy, and sister-in-law to Polly—but to jump in for a second, why are boys and girls allowed in each other's rooms at any time? Who is checking to make sure they're in their dorms at night?

DEAN FISCHER

Well, boys are not allowed in the girls' dorms past eight, and vice versa...

AUNT POLLY

Oh, so they have until eight to make out and Lord knows what else?

DEAN FISCHER

We have cameras!

        The crowd gasps.

DEAN FISCHER (cont.)

In the hallways!

        Virgo turns to Brooklyn.

VIRGO

(Whispering.) Sometimes I think about how many hours of footage there must be of me on surveillance cameras. It could make a nice art project!

DEAN FISCHER

Plus we have dorm advisors, referred to as student life counselors, who are actively involved in—

Mrs. Carmichael stands.

MRS. CARMICHAEL

I was told two of the dorm advisors were recently fired for embezzlement of school funds?

AUNT POLLY

Yeah, and my kid said she once spent a whole day sun tanning. A whole day! Where were the adults to tell her otherwise?! Hello! Cancer, people!

DAISY

What? No, Mom, I'm a Virgo.

VIRGO

Hey, me too! High five!

DEAN FISCHER

Please rest assured that your children are safe and heavily monitored—

AUNT POLLY

What a joke. (Pointing to Dean Fischer, addressing the crowd.) Just look at him, or the other boys! The women are now so *confident* and *smart* that the guys seem helpless in comparison!

MRS. RIVERS

As if male-bashing is fine. It's not. It's comedy rooted in bias and misandry.

DEAN FISCHER

What?! How is this my fault?! (Looking around.) Darren? Mike? What's going—?

MRS. RIVERS

It's the school's emphasis on dating culture, materialism, and a warped sense of self-worth.

DEAN FISCHER

Okay, fine, so the laptop thing, right? Technology in the classroom only serves to aid schools *so long as* access is available to *all students*. It's to close the opportunity gap, as part of our partnership with Temporary Simulations Corporation.

MRS. CARMICHAEL

But that's the thing? That brand names are inescapable? And the sheer amount of commercialism in modern Western culture is unsettling?

DEAN FISCHER

I'm sorry, was there a legitimate question there?

MRS. CARMICHAEL

For our youth, these brand names symbolize unity among a generation whose parents can afford to buy them Whazz energy drinks and Blazer hoverboards, both of which cost dollars more than their cheaper, supposedly generic counterparts?

DEAN FISCHER

(Straightening his tie.) Having sponsored, recognizable product placement grants legitimacy.

MRS. CARMICHAEL

There might be a time and place for such commercialistic hypnosis, yet shouldn't the school setting be free from blatant advertising, lest the institution undermine its students' autonomy as individuals in the digital age?

> Dean Fischer sweats under the California sun. Brooklyn, meanwhile, begins to yawn but quickly corrects this. She blinks twice. She's kept to herself as of late, not letting others into her head. She looks around and then settles on Matthew, who hasn't said anything today. She sees he's not admiring this place full of sunshine and cheer—no, he's focused on the men in suits farther off, watching them watching him, as if just noticing their presence for the first time. She glances away, half asleep, then focuses again on the mothers and the dean. But she does not care, and that's what scares her. She wants to *feel* something. She wants it to hurt.

DEAN FISCHER

We... the board of directors will certainly take that into consideration. Thank you, Miss...

MRS. CARMICHAEL

Yvonne? Carmichael?

> Dean Fischer glares at Chris. He then flashes a polite smile at Mrs. Carmichael, who returns to her seat with Aunt Polly and Mrs. Rivers.

DEAN FISCHER

Does anyone else have a problem with our liberal arts education?

AUNT POLLY

The arts and sciences make us weak!

CHRIS

Oh boy.

AUNT POLLY

Maybe what we need is less science and more conscience!

> Liss rolls her eyes and blows a long raspberry. Brooklyn
> snaps to attention.

LISS

Some of the coolest altruistic things humans have done are completely inseparable from science and technology. There's so much anti-science sentiment out there that it's honestly really sad, and it's not doing anyone any favors!

BROOKLYN

Liss, I wouldn't—

> Liss stands.

LISS

People are so fueled by emotion and are so reactionary—protesting against things without having a clear idea what they're protesting against.

CHRIS

Liss—

LISS

You said you're a farmer, right? Any good farmer knows that treating your sick livestock with veterinary medicine is not only required but more than a good idea. I used to work with rats—

MRS. CARMICHAEL

What do you mean, "work with rats"? As in animal testing?

LISS

Well, yes, but, um, I'm... into art history now. Frida Vinci. Claude Matisse. Andy Pollock, you know, El Salvador. I support animal testing, sure, but I love my rats—

MRS. CARMICHAEL

Um, no? Sorry? Most animal testing is for new makeup or shampoo, of which we have hundreds? If you want to test the effects of something so bad, shouldn't you perform it on someone who can actually consent to it?

Brooklyn turns to Chris.

BROOKLYN

(Whispering.) *What is she doing?!*

LISS

But testing on humans would be infinitely more expensive and time consuming and would carry lots of legal problems—

CHRIS

Mom—

MRS. CARMICHAEL

Rats dream, feel empathy, form friendships, laugh, bond, they're social—
not to mention they're highly intelligent? If you say you like rats but use
them for research and support tests on them, how can you say you like
rats and that you're a good person? It just doesn't make sense?

CHRIS

Mom!

LISS

Science is the very expression of our human curiosity! Why do you
people feel so antagonistic toward it?!

MRS. CARMICHAEL

Because you're not a real rat lover? And you're damaging the cause by
pretending otherwise?

LISS

There... there isn't a dichotomy between science and compassion!

MRS. UNDERWOOD

What a freak.

> Chris turns to Rhys.

CHRIS

(Whispering.) *Dude, say something!*

RHYS

(Whispering back.) *We're not supposed to!*

> Liss pushes back from the table and runs off in tears. Mrs. Carmichael crosses her arms in her chair. Aunt Polly stands again.

AUNT POLLY

The astronauts, poets, painters—they don't deserve our praise! What about the grazers, sowers, and harvesters? The people who *feed* you? Do you even teach agriculture here? Do you not feed our children, Fischer?! (Pointing to Virgo.) Look at her, the skinny twig!

VIRGO

Oh yeah, totally. I never eat anything. Ever. I haven't eaten in decades.

> Mrs. Underwood stands, clapping.

MRS. UNDERWOOD

Yes! Woe is to the farmer, who receives no honor yet keeps us alive! No other profession—such hardship of a lifestyle—directly benefits society more than the farmer!

RHYS

Oh God—

MRS. UNDERWOOD

The farmer's drudgery feeds us while the work of the artist serves to impress us! Does this not seem backward?!

DEAN FISCHER

You… you are an *actor*, Clara! Is no one else seeing the hypocrisy in this?!

MRS. UNDERWOOD

In an effort to stand out, we actors are disingenuous with ourselves and pursue a status of idolatry, whereas those who have true virtue go unrecognized! Sculptors cannot eat their marble, chemists should not drink their chemicals, and musicians, drunk with passion, can certainly try to eat their instruments but will sure look foolish in the process!

DEAN FISCHER

Clara, please. Mrs. Underwood. You've donated tens of thousands of dollars to this school. (Looking around.) You're criticizing the very establishment you're a part of!

Mrs. Rivers crosses her arms.

MRS. RIVERS

Sometimes you have to reach a middle ground.

Brooklyn looks again at Matthew. This time he's staring across the big field at the administration building, by the main entrance to SBA. She doesn't know exactly what he's thinking, but she can imagine, and she imagines it has to do with that afternoon with the hoverboards. It was supposed to be yet another perfect day: a golden-orange sunset behind them, the sound of the Pacific waves in the background, and then Dean Fischer riding his hoverboard, loving it, lifting the ban, and the gang all laughing afterward. Maybe even a beach party.

But that's not what she thinks he sees. She imagines him watching his doppelganger—handsomer, taller, stronger—standing by her side in Dean Fischer's office, this doppelganger kissing her on the cheek, and then Brooklyn looking down to hide her smile, all while Matthew wonders how easily he could be replaced.

If only he knew.

She doesn't like this anymore. She has this burning desire to help him however she can. More action for him, maybe. In the meantime, though, she returns her attention to Mrs. Underwood and Dean Fischer and whatever this is about farming and dissent.

MRS. UNDERWOOD

We are not functioning as citizens when we are so focused with ourselves as a symbol of success! By following this level of competition-based prestige, as does the *elite* and *distinguished* Sea Breeze Academy, our children conform to what they perceive to be others'—or the school's—expectations, memorizing facts for good grades so that they too may one day be as revered as Lita Candyce and Trixie Maltese! Rather than having real, human connections, they maintain personas! And, well, as for my certain Emmy win for Outstanding Guest Actress in a Comedy-Drama Series, I will let the farmers have this victory. Lord knows they don't get enough as it is.

The entire crowd bursts into a standing ovation. Mrs. Underwood turns around, performs a curtsy, and then returns to her seat, as does Aunt Polly. The applause continues. Brooklyn fidgets in her chair. Dean Fischer sighs.

DEAN FISCHER

Folks, please. Hear me out! Sea Breeze Academy is about... setting a good mood. A carefree enjoyment of life! We want to empower our youth, to change lives, to touch children!

AUNT POLLY

The heck?

DEAN FISCHER

Girl Power! Cool with a capital C! We're providing these kids an escape from reality. Let them have it! It's about reflecting the importance of having good—albeit photogenic—friends by your side. It's not about the accuracy to a more... well, a regular boarding school experience. If you want realism, go check out the History Channel! This place is about a chance at freedom, a chance at self-autonomy! SBA is not a normal school!

MRS. CARMICHAEL

Oh, so this isn't a school? It's a theme park?!

MRS. RIVERS

Escapism isn't sustainable.

> Brooklyn blinks and stands and faces the crowd, her honeyed hair blowing in the breeze, the warmth of the California sun on her face like a spotlight.

BROOKLYN

Hi, everyone. My name is Brooklyn Rivers, and I'm a junior at Sea

Breeze Academy. Applying here was honestly the greatest decision I've ever made for myself. I *love* this school. The people and the professors here are amazing, and everything is more laid-back than where I was previously living. SBA is just an all-around awesome place to start a new chapter in your life—

MRS. CARMICHAEL

And she leads everyone on all these dangerous exploits? And so we get to hear about all the protests happening at this school, the shenanigans, that freaky "curse of SBA" with all the graves that were dug up on Halloween—?

CHRIS

Mom, for real though, nothing all that spooky has ever happened to me here. (Beat.) There is a huge cistern under our dorm that's full of animal skulls and heptagrams, so that's a thing, but other than that—

DEAN FISCHER

Please, Chris, stop. Please.

MRS. UNDERWOOD

We pledge allegiance to the kids!

> The audience cheers once more and tosses confetti high into the air. Dean Fischer looks down and rubs his temples for several moments, his elbows on the podium. He scowls at the trouble table.

DEAN FISCHER

All right. All right! Fine. You win. I'm going for a walk. Class dismissed.

Dean Fischer exits the stage. Denzel approaches with a cameraman for an interview, but the dean shoves the camera out of his face. Aunt Polly looks around.

AUNT POLLY

Well, I'm down for seconds. Who's coming with?

The kids, except Matthew, laugh, as do the mothers. They rise to rejoin the food line. Brooklyn glances around for Liss, but she's nowhere to be seen. The weather is perfect, the ocean is calm, and also, it's time for a commercial.

* * *

Back at Sea Breeze Academy, Matthew sits alone at one of the tables. He grips his phone, the new TSC Dreamscape GX Prime S Plus Close-Parenthesis or another. He passes it back and forth between each hand, then places it on the table. He leaves it there. More important, it turns out the mothers all went to the same college together, and each dated a young Dean Fischer; naturally, chaos ensues.

On their way to the drama, Chris and Tina walk by Matthew hand in hand. They notice him. They stop at his table.

CHRIS

Hey, man. How's it going?

MATTHEW

Oh, you know.

CHRIS

I don't. That's why I asked. Why so glum, chum?

MATTHEW

I don't feel well.

CHRIS

Ah. One too many burgers?

MATTHEW

What? No, not... no. It's bigger than that.

CHRIS

So... *two* too many burgers?

TINA

Maybe Matthew needs some alone time, babe.

CHRIS

Is that true? Is that what you need? Do you need a drink of water?

> Matthew shrugs. Tina crosses her arms, a look of concern in her eyes. Chris takes a nearby seat.

CHRIS (cont.)

We should play basketball again sometime. Without you, it was just Rhys and me, for the most part, and the boy can't jump to save his life.

202 BRYANT A. LONEY

(Smiling.) Or we could go down to the beach, you know?

MATTHEW

The men in the suits and sunglasses—have they always been there? Watching?

CHRIS

Hey, whoa, careful now. Ixnay on the enmay.

MATTHEW

Ixnay on the enmay? (Beat.) Atwhay oday ouyay eanmay?

CHRIS

Eway ouldshay alktay… about… omethingsay ifferentday.

MATTHEW

What about… parlez-vous français?

Chris shakes his head.

CHRIS

No. You heard the moms. There needs to be changes, and there have been, and there will be. Things will get better.

MATTHEW

But there are other, better solutions than the enmay. They could open administrative meetings to students to increase transparency, for starters. Keep the library open later for studying. Have more widely dispersed announcements about activities and clubs, increase access to hygiene products on campus… (Laughing to himself.) Oh, but why would anybody listen to me? What even was that earlier, with the moms?

CHRIS

Look, man. I'm sorry I haven't been there for you as much as before. I've wanted to, but we've been so busy, and I've got this thing later with Siddiq—you know how it is.

MATTHEW

And Liss?

CHRIS

It's not right, if that's what you mean. Liss is great. Girl cracks me up. But Matthew, *you're* my best friend. You and each of your freckles. We'll catch up soon, okay? I wanna know all about you and Brooklyn and everything about Alaska. And I know you're a funny guy who likes to do his own thing—I get that—but for now, keep it basic. All right? Channel that humor you're known for. If you ignore the crazy, the crazy goes away.

MATTHEW

Sure. Of course.

CHRIS

Cool. I'll see you later.

TINA

Bye, Matthew.

> Chris stands, and then he and Tina leave, hand in hand again. Matthew frowns. They should all be soaking up

some sun at this big round table. Together. That's what they would have done before. He doesn't get blurry vision, and there isn't the strum of a harp or anything, but this, at least, he remembers.

Someone calls out Matthew's name. He looks up to see a generic white man approaching him. The man has drawn-on freckles and wears an executive business suit. This is "Matthew's Dad."

"MATTHEW'S DAD"

Hey, champ. This seat taken?

MATTHEW

Huh? Oh, no. Go ahead.

"Matthew's Dad" sits beside him.

"MATTHEW'S DAD"

You remember me. Right, son?

MATTHEW

What? Why wouldn't I? We had that video chat last year. When I needed advice with Brooklyn.

"MATTHEW'S DAD"

That's right. So why isn't your girlfriend here with you?

MATTHEW

She's with her family—her mom, cousin, and aunt.

"MATTHEW'S DAD"

Things good between you two?

MATTHEW

Maybe? I don't know. It's been… strange. I'm trying to just deal with it.

"MATTHEW'S DAD"

That's smart. I like your thinking.

MATTHEW

It's something at least.

> Matthew and "Matthew's Dad" sit quietly. At another table are three moms chatting.

FAKE-ACCENT MOM

Just bought Mykelti her first car—a Luxur Y-BS convertible, only the best for my little girl—and she started yelling because she can't drive it until she gets her license! Kids are *so* ungrateful. I said she couldn't go out to the movies or whatever for the next *five weeks* until she changes her attitude.

NASAL-VOICE MOM

Kymbyrlyn is the same way. She broke her brand-new phone while having a temper tantrum—all because she wanted to have a "real dessert like all the other kids" instead of my organic whole wheat gluten-free and non-GMO fruit bread. It's almost twice as expensive as the toxic GMO waste food products, but it's sooooo worth it! Oh, how I *love* being upper-class! I can't believe all those poor people!

206 BRYANT A. LONEY

THE "I'D LIKE TO SPEAK TO YOUR MANAGER" MOM

Hey, other moms, I need some advice. Lakaylyleigh's teachers aren't pronouncing her name correctly in class, and she was just so upset today, she didn't even eat her quinoa! All because I liked the unique spelling! It's obviously pronounced "Mary," but they're not grasping the concept. Do I contact the school board?

FAKE-ACCENT MOM

My son Jayceyn and my other daughter Britkneigh were fighting earlier today over who gets to take our hypercar and who has to take the supercar to their vegan salsa-and-seltzer-tasting party tonight. Kids these days! It's like they can't just take the limo and shut up!

"MATTHEW'S DAD"

Son.

> Matthew is pulled back to attention.

"MATTHEW'S DAD" (cont.)

Your dean asked me to speak with you. Says you've been acting up lately. What do you think?

MATTHEW

Well, I… things have been weird. Different. I guess things aren't so much the same as before. And I'm not trying to be, like, inflexible or anything. It should be a perfectly good day.

> Matthew takes a deep breath of fresh Pacific air, windless
> and warm. He holds it in his lungs, listens to the playing
> music, to the ocean, imagines the sound of him breathing,

the sound of the oysters, hauntingly silent in the infinite darkness, trailing fire, wilting into atoms, withering into space dust, and he waits one more second, and then he lets it all out slowly.

MATTHEW (cont.)

I can best describe it as a void that I know exists and that I try so hard to keep my attention from. But then I also feel compelled to look into it. And it sucks me in.

"MATTHEW'S DAD"

Let me stop you there, champ. Remember that time when you were four or five and we were practicing baseball in the backyard? We were both standing, facing each other, and I was telling you that after you hit the ball, you run to the right—and I pointed right? You, in front of me, pointed to your right and said, but this is right. And we stood there arguing for a good half hour on which way was right. And we were both right! It was just our different perspectives. All is as it is perceived.

MATTHEW

Yes! So you're saying my perspective is valid!

"MATTHEW'S DAD"

Valid, sure, but not valuable. This is America, so you're allowed to have an opinion on anything you'd like—raise the flag and put your hand on your heart. But does your opinion bring any real value to the discussion? Not really, no. It also doesn't mean you're not allowed to be part of the discussion. But it's better to listen than talk. The greatest talent one can have is learning when to speak and when to not. Or being talented at learning new talents. Like acting. You could try elevating your ignorance into an art form, where your lack of knowledge in itself proves a point.

MATTHEW

So, like that saying, ignorance is bliss.

"MATTHEW'S DAD"

If not bliss, then at least less work. Soon it shall also be art.

> "Matthew's Dad" turns to briefly admire the bright and bold SBA flag waving triumphantly in the warm California breeze.

"MATTHEW'S DAD" (cont.)

SBA used to be an all-white school, you know. It's true! Not because we banned other races from joining, but that's just how it worked. Then we started looking for black people specifically, but just one at a time. Then Latinos. Then Asians. Now Yuranis. We don't discrimize.

MATTHEW

My head hurts, and I have this feeling in my stomach that—

"MATTHEW'S DAD"

There you go again. Son, do you feel as if you don't deserve friends? A good life? Is that why you've isolated yourself? You have control over your emotions. They shouldn't have control over you. Happiness is just being able to accept a lot of things as they happen across your path. Television shows are a good substitute for happiness. They work well enough. And one day soon, you'll be so content with your unhappiness that you'll get into the groove of it, and then you'll reach a state of

Zen-like contentment.

> Matthew feels the blood pounding in his temples. He wipes the sweat from his forehead.

MATTHEW

Fine. Okay. Let's pretend you're right. So what should I do—now that I realize my problems are fake and that I've been such a terrible, *terrible* person this whole time?

> "Matthew's Dad" pulls out a folded piece of paper. He hands it to Matthew.

"MATTHEW'S DAD"

I'm glad you ask. Take this. Read these lines, memorize them, and then deliver 'em to your friends by the end of the day. Put energy into it! I need you to reek of pizzazz, son. Got it?

> "Matthew's Dad" stands, pops his back, and then puts a hand on Matthew's shoulder. He smiles, completely businesslike.

"MATTHEW'S DAD" (cont.)

One more thing. You are swimming farther and farther out to sea, Matthew, and beyond are blind, pale, *cricket-like* monsters at the edge of reality. They are twitching, their mandibles gnashing, crawling all over each other, spreading their scorch marks and infestation beneath black, howling stars. They were children once. Not anymore. They are demonic. And they are sensing you. And they are waiting. And you do not want to meet them. (Beat.) Don't forget the pizzazz!

"Matthew's Dad" walks away, fading into the shimmering heat. Matthew scratches his neck.

Seagulls fly overhead into the darkening blue of the sky. Matthew sighs. He opens the piece of paper, reads, frowns, and then tries the words on his lips. Above all, he wants his friends to like him again. He's not sure how it ever got so crazy. But he's willing to do his part to fix it.

Later, in the distance, Matthew sees Brooklyn, Virgo, Chris, and Rhys walking without him. He pockets his lines, then hurries over to catch up to them.

VIRGO

Hey, Matthew.

CHRIS

What's up?

Matthew leans his weight first on one foot and then the other.

MATTHEW

So guys. I just stopped and realized that this... this *general anxiety* and discontent and doom... is actually all in my head.

Brooklyn and Chris smile at this, urging him on.

MATTHEW (cont.)

Yeah, I know. You'd think that it would've come sooner, but it didn't seem like a concrete fact up until this point. And in some ways, I need to change things so that this doesn't happen again. (Laughing too loud too quickly.) I'd probably be less annoying to everybody that way. I guess I see now that I likely have a lot of life in store, and it's probably gonna be filled with a lot of good and a lot of bad, and that's normal, and I should stop bothering people with it. And—and if you too ever have a moment like this, I recommend you do as I have done and take the time to stop and hold the universe in your hands, to see the stars colliding in your palms. Honestly, I can't remember the last time I felt this healthy and clear-headed. It seems so weird to me now how I've been trapped in my own head for all this time, not even noticing how ridiculous I looked feeling like nothing was okay for the past couple of weeks. So I've decided to stop being so sad and... (Pausing for just the right amount of time.) Be wildly happy and full of light and energy and love instead.

He finishes. The group smiles.

BROOKLYN

That's all we needed to hear.

RHYS

I'm happy for you, man.

VIRGO

Same. I hope this freeing revelation continues for you forever!

MATTHEW

Thanks, you guys.

CHRIS

You coming with us for sushi?

Brooklyn takes Matthew's hand. He looks at her. She smiles and then he smiles, a semi-restored light in their eyes. Matthew doesn't need to answer Chris. He's getting sushi with them for the rest of the semester, even if it kills him.

The gang walks together, joking and laughing and cloud gazing in unison. The breeze is light. Life is great. All is well.

A perfect ending to another perfect day. A bird's eye view of Sea Breeze Academy, and then the credits roll.

1. Hey Brando.
2. Go.
1. Good work there buddy.
2. Thanks.

"UNDERWOOD'S UNDERWEAR"

Rhys convinces Dean Fischer to have Sea Breeze Academy host a fashion show with SBA students as the models.

Another perfect day in Southern California. Virgo, Chris, Rhys, and Matthew sit at their familiar lunch table outside Zhang Hall, with a view over the California foothills to the ocean below. The Pacific sunshine is warm and comforting. Virgo frowns, her phone in her hands.

VIRGO

I just can't believe this guy never texted me back. I mean, I deleted him on all my social media accounts and told him to never contact me again... but I'm surprised he actually listened to me!

CHRIS

Maybe he's just doing what you said to do?

RHYS

(Rolling his eyes.) Girls. Always saying one thing and meaning the other.

VIRGO

I don't know.

> Brooklyn, looking fatigued, trudges over to the rounded
> lunch table and droops into the nearest seat. She runs
> her hands through her hair, brushing it out of her face.

VIRGO (cont.)

Hey, roomie.

CHRIS

Yo.

RHYS

'Sup?

BROOKLYN

Hey, guys. *Whew!* Sorry. I set my alarm for really early this morning
so I could go running, but I guess it didn't go off, so I was late to
pre-calc—even with my hoverboard. (Her head in her hands.) Mr. Del
Mar's gonna give me an F for the day if I'm late again.

> Rhys scoffs, then flexes in his sleeveless SBA hoodie.

RHYS

Math class. Gross. Only pseudo-intellectual idiots like math. Last
year, I bought two thousand calculators just so two thousand children
would have to go without. I hate math. I hate it!

CHRIS

Math's not for everybody, but it can be fun for some. (Sheepishly adjusting his eyepatch.) I like math...

RHYS

Whoa, "math" and "fun" in the same sentence. Please explain.

VIRGO

Just the mentioning of math can be enough to make me cry.

RHYS

I can hardly read clocks!

MATTHEW

Well, if it helps, a lot of math doesn't involve clocks.

> Rhys sighs. He sits with one arm slung over the back of his seat.

RHYS

Brooklyn, Virgo, is there a polite way to tell someone they're being a sassypants? Could I just say "sassypants"? There're so many things you can't say anymore...

BROOKLYN

"You're being a sassypants."

VIRGO

"No offense, but you're being a humongously rude sassypants."

RHYS

Great, so we all agree "sassypants" is perfect.

BROOKLYN

Painfully perfect.

Rhys turns to Matthew.

RHYS

You, sir, are being a sassypants.

VIRGO

Sassypants!

CHRIS

(Pointing.) Ha-ha! Sassypants!

The whole gang, except Matthew, laughs.

RHYS

My point is, clocks have numbers, and fancy clocks have letters, and those are the worst. They're torture devices!

CHRIS

Man, math can be cool. Like... doing derivatives and integrals can be nice after hours of reading dusty old English books about sad old men. It's exercise for the brain!

VIRGO

Cardio is exercise. Not math.

RHYS

Chris is clearly a math apologist. Still, you gotta be nice to math nerds because they're the ones who run the economy. Math only exists so people can count their money and their debts. (Beat.) Hey, Matthew, what time is it?

> Matthew looks at his bare arm.

MATTHEW

XII-LIV o'clock.

> Rhys stands up to fight, but Chris pulls him back down
> by the shoulder.

CHRIS

Look, if you're never gonna use math in your adult life, that's limiting a whole lotta options for yourself.

VIRGO

Yeah, Rhys, what'll you be doing ten years from now? Other than watching me and your mom on the red carpet together.

CHRIS

Yeah, you're not gonna live off Mommy Underwood forever, are you?

RHYS

Um, no!

CHRIS

Gonna go to college? Gonna major in something?

VIRGO

He'll probably choose something weird like black magick with a minor in hexes.

BROOKLYN

Sounds exotic.

MATTHEW

Sounds expensive.

RHYS

All right, all right, enough already! Jeez! (Taking a breath.) So we all know that growing up is a trap and we agree never to do it. But, if we're being serious for a second... I've, well, I've always wanted to design women's underclothes and then host a modeling show based off it. I think it'd be fun.

Matthew stares at Rhys in disbelief.

MATTHEW

You... you want to make women's bras and panties?

Chris snorts.

CHRIS

Heh. "Panties."

VIRGO

I think it's a great idea.

BROOKLYN

Yeah, who's to say men can't be into fashion?

CHRIS

Plus you have so much experience with women's underwear.

MATTHEW

Good God.

BROOKLYN

I bet you Dean Fischer would even let you have it here at the school if you refer to it as an extracurricular. It'd be SBA's first fashion show!

MATTHEW

Uhh, guys, hello? Aren't modeling shows kind of sexist?

RHYS

Okay, Mr. Politically Correct, thanks for your contribution. Real happy we asked you!

BROOKLYN

No, it's good of Matthew to be thoughtful, even if looking after us like that is kind of overstepping.

MATTHEW

What?

RHYS

Shush it, General Blah.

Brooklyn, Virgo, and Chris laugh. Matthew joins in at his expense.

CHRIS

Heh. "General Blah."

MATTHEW

Am I a mister or a general? Or am I still a sassypants?

RHYS

You're annoying is what you are.

CHRIS

Dude.

BROOKLYN

We're confident in our bodies, Matthew, and that's our right as twenty-first-century women. What you're thinking of is beauty pageants or any other type of event where women compete against each other and get points for "construction of the head" or whatever. This is more of a... a celebration of clothing.

CHRIS

Or lack thereof.

MATTHEW

Stop that.

CHRIS

And you could even use students as models!

VIRGO

Oh my God, yes, I would love to be a model. Can you imagine what that would do for my résumé if I were in a fashion show? I'd get talent agents everywhere! Hiding under benches, licking my feet when I sit—

MATTHEW

Brooklyn, you wouldn't seriously consider modeling underwear for Rhys, would you?

BROOKLYN

Well... I don't know... it could be fun?

RHYS

You *would* look great in some underclothing.

> Brooklyn glares at Rhys. He holds up his hands defensively.

RHYS (cont.)

Joking! I mean, you would. But I meant it in a jestful way. It's playful! For grins! A knee-slapper!

BROOKLYN

Oh, it's a something-slapper all right.

CHRIS

Modeling could be good experience for you girls. You too, Rhys— *finally* you'll have *something* to put on your college applications besides basketball, volleyball, baseball, golf, track, wrestling, tennis, surfing, water polo...

RHYS

Did you mention I'm handsome?

CHRIS

I think we know that. (Shaking his head.) See, SBA just doesn't bring anything extra to the table. Not anymore. It's all been done, and better. You heard the moms complaining. So what I say we do is let Rhys have his modeling show, get the school involved, have it televised, and then sell the rights for an animated series. We'll build a mobile app that caters to the younger generation, get some merch, capitalize off the nostalgia in ten years...

BROOKLYN

Appealing to nostalgia can only take you so far. People move on.

VIRGO

We have to be fresh, new, and exciting.

RHYS

So it's settled then. You all in?

BROOKLYN

I am!

VIRGO

Hecks yeah!

MATTHEW

You're not busy, Virgo? With work?

VIRGO

Oh yeah, the store closed. We were all laid off.

MATTHEW

Why?! What happened to the bookstore?!

VIRGO

The Internet happened.

RHYS

Duh.

CHRIS

I'll go talk to Tina about modeling.

BROOKLYN

Virgo, we have to get to class.

Brooklyn faces Matthew.

BROOKLYN (cont.)

Can you talk to Liss about all this? Maybe give her that speech of yours that cured you of your depression? She's in our room, sick or something.

MATTHEW

Sure, I can... do that.

BROOKLYN

Cool, thanks. (Standing up.) See you, dudes!

RHYS

See *you* in your underpants!

> Brooklyn and Virgo stand to leave, but Brooklyn first kisses Matthew on the cheek before taking off. Matthew blushes. Rhys leans back, his hands behind his head. He grins.

RHYS (cont.)

You guys know I don't actually want to design clothes when I'm older, right?

> Chris laughs.

CHRIS

Oh yeah. You'll be living off your trust fund till the day you die.

MATTHEW

So what was that all about?

RHYS

Dude, our lady friends are hot. You're lucky you got Brooklyn. Brooklyn's hardcore. *Whew!*

CHRIS

Whew indeed!

MATTHEW

This seems wrong.

RHYS

Your face seems wrong! What even are freckles?

MATTHEW

A result of overproduction of melanin?

RHYS

Signs of reptilian ancestry, more like.

CHRIS

Think about it this way: prospective students are touring, right? If they see how hot the girls are here, more kids will come to SBA, the school will get more funding, and things'll be better off for everybody!

MATTHEW

And by "hot," you mean what? Like, are you allowing plus-size models?

RHYS

What fat people do you see around here? There are way too many stairs for that. It's SoCal! You think people go this school for the academics? Our sports? Please. Any fat person, we shamed away a long time ago.

CHRIS

Or put on a strict diet...

Chris holds his belly, frowning.

RHYS

Anyway... you dudes shut up while I call my mom.

Rhys takes out his phone. He taps the screen, then holds it up to his ear.

RHYS (cont.)

Hey, Mom, how's—? Yeah? ... Okay, yeah. Sorry... So I was wondering, could I throw a modeling event here on campus? I'd have to get Dean Fischer's permission, but I wanted to check with you to see... Yeah, the platinum card. Uh-huh... More like sleepwear, underwear, that kind of... Ivy's Innuendo?! Cool! Great! ... Love you, Mom— ... Sorry, sorry. *Mrs. Underwood*. Bye.

Rhys ends the call.

MATTHEW

What'd she say?

RHYS

That you give off a fedora vibe.

MATTHEW

Huh?

CHRIS

A fed-*aura!*

RHYS

Momma didn't raise no fool!

MATTHEW

Momma raised a weirdo.

RHYS

Whatever. Now I have to talk to the dean. Wish me luck!

CHRIS

Luck, bro!

Somewhere between that beach and that sky, Rhys leaves, as does Chris. Matthew sits alone, going over what he should have said, staring solemnly at the ocean in the distance. So many lunches at this spot. He remembers Brooklyn suggesting the table almost five semesters ago. Simpler times. Terrible fashion, but simpler times. Matthew laughs to himself. He would always wear these long-sleeve button-downs, and Brooklyn, a tank top over her t-shirt. At least his friends weren't arguing as much back then. At least he wasn't so sad all the time. No random product endorsements, no props, no secret meetings, no men in suits. Nothing like that, and certainly no slapping of former roommates.

He waits a little while longer. Finally, he gets up to leave, and also, it's time for a commercial.

* * *

Back at Sea Breeze Academy, Matthew knocks on the door to Room 102 in Dutton Suites. He waits. More important, Rhys has just finished convincing Dean Fischer to let SBA host the modeling show, and Brooklyn and Virgo are participating in a workout sequence so that they'll look their best for the night's event.

Matthew opens the door. The lights are off, the curtains are closed, and Liss lies on the bottom bunk with a damp rag on her forehead and a cup of tea beside her. She looks over at Matthew, groans, and rolls over. Matthew shuts the door behind him.

MATTHEW

Hey, Liss. How are you?

LISS

Just leave me alone.

Matthew sits beside the bed.

MATTHEW

Brooklyn said you weren't feeling well.

LISS

Ha. She said that, huh? She's destructive, you know. Desperate. I doubt she even knows the capital of Oklahoma.

Liss rolls over to face him.

LISS (cont.)

I feel like a part of me is missing, as if a section of my brain has shut off.

MATTHEW

Stroke?

LISS

No. It's just a weird feeling I get. "Depersonalization" would be the best way to describe it. I ruin everything because of my stupid anxiety. And then my stomach ruins everything because I ruin everything because of my stupid anxiety. It's weird having friends but not being able to talk about your feelings with them because you're so far out there. So, as together as you are, you're also alone.

MATTHEW

What does that mean?

LISS

I don't know, Matthew. I am but a yogurt-covered pretzel in the void. Sweet on the outside, salty on the inside, and always deceiving people into thinking I'm not that bad when I'm actually packed with calories and trans fats.

MATTHEW

That... doesn't help me understand, whatever it was you said.

She sits up.

LISS

Do you remember the classes you took last year? Do you? What about two years ago? Do you remember your schedule that semester?

MATTHEW

Not off the top of my head, no.

LISS

So how do you know you had classes at all?

MATTHEW

I remember certain teachers, specific lessons, days, some moments...

LISS

So particular instances stood out to you. And the rest of the time, you spent doing...?

MATTHEW

It all just sort of runs together.

LISS

So based on memorable events—all spread out—from a handful of teachers, you assume you received an education.

MATTHEW

Right.

LISS

But ironically, you don't remember most of it.

MATTHEW

Do you?

LISS

This isn't about me.

MATTHEW

But no one can remember everything.

LISS

You're right. This is true. With the information we gather, sensory or otherwise, we seek patterns. We connect imaginary dots. So tell me. What did you eat for dinner last Tuesday?

MATTHEW

What? I don't know. I don't even know what day it is. I barely know what month it is.

LISS

So did you eat?

MATTHEW

I believe so, yes.

LISS

But can you be a hundred percent certain if you don't—if you *cannot* remember it?

MATTHEW

I guess the answer is no.

LISS

It's easy to assume you ate dinner last Tuesday. What's hard is to admit you're not sure that you did.

MATTHEW

I have a feeling this isn't about food.

LISS

No, Matthew! God, can't you see this?! How weird everything is?! What we say must be truth, because why else would we say it? It's like… this continuous internal screaming. It makes me nervous how limited my frame of understanding is, and I have this constant anxiety that I don't have long to live and that I… won't be able to stop it. And I know my age, but when someone asks me how old I am, I still have to think for a while. Sometimes for a long time. Same with my name, occasionally. These worries—they're always on my mind, even if they're just in the background. We used to be so close. All of us. Before kids were taken away in the back of vans and high school girls had to model lingerie.

MATTHEW

You know about that?

LISS

Of course I do. It's all I'm good for at this point. They forget I'm still smart. They didn't want the science nerd girl to make fun of anymore, so they dressed me up and tossed out my glasses and gave me a girliness upgrade so I'd look more like you all. So I'd look normal. Something in the Whazz, maybe. Hypnotic suggestions? Stupidity-inducing, mind-altering chemicals? Pheromone manipulation? All I have left is my body and Lewis and Wistar, and they're not even the same rats as before. We've gone through three of each! Half the time, they're just puppets, anyway. God, if PETA found out, they'd kill us.

MATTHEW

And Brooklyn?

LISS

What, are you asking if this is one of her manic episodes? That thing, with her and Miki—total out-of-the-blue moment. With Brooklyn, it's like you're playing with fire. She's using you. So watch yourself.

MATTHEW

You lost me, Liss.

LISS

You left! Don't you get it?! If you're gone, stay gone!

> Liss stands, crying softly.

LISS (cont.)

But here you are. The thing, with the Pulov kid—

> An alarm sounds. Liss and Matthew turn to Brooklyn's nightstand, where her clock beeps increasingly louder with each passing second. Liss clicks it off.

LISS (cont.)

That's not normal. Neither are blank books, wearing hijabs for the sake of it, and former students sneaking around like refugees in some war. Listen to me closely, Matthew: *it's reasonable to believe a claim to be false when there is no reason to believe it to be true.* Individuals do not establish knowledge. Groups do. It's all a big show! What we're doing here—it's deliberate deception.

The alarm sounds again. Liss grabs it, opens a window, and then flings it outside. A cat meows in pain.

LISS (cont.)

And you know what—I am *done* doing this, I am *fed up* with being someone's puppet! So I'm not going up on that stage in my bra and underwear. That's where I draw the line. I don't know what they'll tell you or where they're gonna say I transferred to, but I'm not doing it. Not this time. I've been humiliated long enough. One day, you'll see it too.

Liss exits the room before Matthew can say anything more. On the bed, she's left behind Lewis and Wistar, which are in fact two white socks with buttons for eyes. Matthew sighs. He remembers once, a year or so ago, when Virgo and Brooklyn were arguing—something about the music volume or sharing clothes or the AC. Typical roommate drama. And Matthew just sat there with Liss, watching, while Wistar stood up in his cage, squinted, and then slowly crawled up into his hammock and slept. Smart rat.

Matthew takes another look around this box of a room. A lot of it's changed over the years. The personality's gone. Black flies on the windowsill, a dead cricket in the corner, the SBA hoodie that Brooklyn's had for years, filled with holes and falling apart at the seams. These memories of theirs.

He goes over to Brooklyn's bed, feels the sheets with the palm of his hand. She's beautiful. Brooklyn. He's loved her since the day he fell into that fountain.

They had a good thing going. He misses that. So, so much. They were best friends once upon a time. Sure, there were issues with Sea Breeze Academy, but back then, they would at least focus more on the solution than the problem. That's what made it interesting. But now—now it's time for a commercial, and Matthew can't help but cry.

* * *

Back at Sea Breeze Academy, Rhys Underwood's Flight of Fancy Intimate Things Extravaganza is well underway at Jackson Commons, which is surrounded by steel security fencing. In front of the raised stage are over two hundred students dressed in formalwear, with Chris, Rhys, and Dean Fischer in the front row. Onstage, Denzel Davis serves as the emcee, his camera crew filming live for *SBA News*. The set is designed in reds and pinks, with the main feature being a lit runway down the middle and into the cheering crowd.

Bedroom pop blasts from the sound system. The sun is lower in the sky, flashing a luminous orange over the tranquil Pacific Ocean. Conveniently, there's a front-row seat next to Chris. Matthew takes it.

CHRIS

Hey, man. You're just in time.

MATTHEW

And Tina was cool with this? With her being up there?

CHRIS

Oh. Uhh, no, not really. (Beat.) Okay, not at all. She's out. She said this was the final straw—

DENZEL

And now, ladies and gentlemen, please welcome to the stage SBA junior and aspiring actress Victoria "Virgo" Torres, as hot as the desert sun!

> Rhys and Chris clap as Virgo struts down the runway in an *Arabian Nights* lingerie costume, featuring a sheer blue bralette with gold coin detailing, a matching thong, a gold armband, and a sheer blue face mask and headpiece with gold trim. Beneath it all, Virgo appears unhealthily thin, almost to the bone. Several guys catcall her through the applause. She blows them kisses.

MATTHEW

Oh my God. She looks—

RHYS

Great! She looks great, dude! *Whew!*

> Rhys places the event's program over his lap as he claps harder for Virgo. Matthew turns to face the dean.

MATTHEW

Dean Fischer?

DEAN FISCHER

What he said! This is great! Do you know how many people are streaming us live right now? Four point five million! We're all the buzz! You got *Hollywood's Highest* talking about us, *VERTEX* magazine—hell, even those cheap pageview sites like *Masterbait*. I just hope they show their feet. (Running a hand through his hair.) Our assets are cooked, you know. Thank God for Ivy's Innuendo.

MATTHEW

The women's lingerie company?

DEAN FISCHER

Yeah, to be honest, I don't know what we'd do without the money. 'Cause while things are awesome as usual here, off campus, not so much. For instance, right now, we have the Women Against Fashion Shows group protesting out by the main entrance, plus the Men Against Women Protesting protestors, who for some reason showed up first? The Handicap Accessibility Awareness group is out there on account of the school not having a lot of ramps, and thus no students in wheelchairs. But they're hard to see past the Protestants Against Protesting non-protestors, who are handing out cardigans and are actually campus police. The secret police are on holiday. Also, the Actor's Union. It's a lot to keep track of.

> Dean Fischer's phone rings in his jacket pocket. He takes it out and checks the text. He frowns.

DEAN FISCHER (cont.)

Oh crud.

MATTHEW

What is it?

DEAN FISCHER

It's your friend Liss, the rat girl. She tried stealing a utility truck. Didn't get very far—doesn't know how to drive. Me, wearing a tie—you'd think I know what I'm doing. But anyway. We caught her. What a mess. (Turning to Matthew.) And stop asking so many questions! You're making it difficult. You're like the son I never wanted—and I already have one of those.

MATTHEW

What?!

DENZEL

Next up, well, she only does everything. Put your hands together for your academic overachiever, environmental activist, straw feminist, class president, Miss Fanservice herself... Brooklyn Rivers!

> Brooklyn saunters toward the audience in a seductive Hollywood black and red open-cup bra—revealing her nipples—and a crotchless lace panty with an open rear and mini bow detail. Her hips sway like the palm trees and flowers. She waves at the whistling boys. Rhys fingers his collar.

RHYS

Whoa.

CHRIS

Yeah. Whoa. (Patting Matthew's shoulder.) Hey, man... how you doing?

MATTHEW

I'm... feeling a little lightheaded.

> Brooklyn hops off the stage and walks over to Matthew, her back straight and shoulders high. She leans in front of him, her legs around the seat, her hands firm on his shoulders as she lowers herself into his lap. Matthew flinches. She then rubs her hands over her tanned skin, touching herself, her head back, his eyes darting around but always settling for more than a moment on her waist. She clutches his face with two hands and then kisses him, deep and passionate and smelling of citrus. He feels the softness of her lips against his own. The crowd goes wild. She leans in to whisper.

BROOKLYN

Meet me at my place at eight.

> Brooklyn tousles Matthew's hair. She then stands, smiling, and she's helped by Denzel back onto the stage. The audience screams Brooklyn and Matthew's names, hailing the duo's star-crossed will-they-or-won't-they? love for each other. She exits stage left.

RHYS

Dude!

CHRIS

Oh. My. God.

MATTHEW

Wow.

RHYS

"Wow"?! You have Brooklyn Rivers giving you a lap dance in front of the entire school and all you can think to say is "Wow"?!

MATTHEW

Oh wow... wow? Double wow?!

RHYS

Jeez, dude, if you're not gonna appreciate your lady, lend her over to me for the night. God.

DENZEL

Thank you, Brooklyn! And lucky Matthew. Yay for Team Mattlyn! And I'd just like to take a moment to thank God for this opportunity: thank you, Lord. Now let's give it up for Brooklyn's younger cousin, fourteen-year-old freshman Daisy "Double D" Rivers, who's currently in a throuple with Tauj'zah and ☺!

> Daisy steps out in a multi-strapped black bandage bra and a matching panty with a keyhole cutout, thigh-high stockings, a black vinyl collar, and wrist restraints. She waves around a leash in one hand and carries a pole with the other. She strides forward, the audience watching her every move, the pout of her lower lip. Daisy then sets the pole in an insert on the stage and begins to step around and hook the pole with her leg. She arches her body as she swings. Chris flips up his eye patch. The crowd goes

wild once more.

AUNT POLLY

Fourteen! Fourteen!

DAISY

Mom?!

> Aunt Polly abruptly pulls herself onto the stage and then rips the pole out from the ground, threatening to beat Daisy with it. Instead, she points it at Denzel, who backs away with his hands in the air.

AUNT POLLY

She is *fourteen years of age! Fourteen!* And you clowns have her up here in her... her unmentionables?!

> She raises the pole. Denzel cowers, his arms crossed in front of him as if that would suppress the blow. Aunt Polly tosses the pole to the side and points a stern finger into Daisy's face.

AUNT POLLY (cont.)

In the car! Now! We are *done* with this crackpot school!

> Dean Fischer walks onto the stage.

DEAN FISCHER

Miss Rivers, please, let's groupthink this!

Aunt Polly cracks her knuckles, shoulders, and neck, and then kicks the dean between the legs. He falls to the floor, and the crowd gasps.

DEAN FISCHER (cont.)

Sec... security! (Coughing.) Security, over here!

AUNT POLLY

"Security" this, ya hackneyed freak!

Aunt Polly gets down and starts hitting Dean Fischer in the side. He cries out in pain with each jab, his shrieks weaving in and out with the awful sound of fist meeting flesh. Dean Fischer rocks himself back and forth, sobbing. Denzel steps up to the mic.

DENZEL

See, I've been told to "roll with the punches," but *that's* just ridiculous!

The audience laughs. Dean Fischer grumbles. The men in suits arrive to remove Aunt Polly—kicking and screaming—from the stage. Daisy, mortified, runs after them, the leash trailing behind her as she whines and whines about wanting to be famous.

DENZEL (cont.)

Well, folks, that's our show! Reporting to you live from Robert Jackson Commons, covering the news that matters, I'm Denzel Davis. This is *SBA News*. And now, the commercials.

* * *

Back at Sea Breeze Academy, Matthew stands outside Brooklyn's dorm room in Dutton Suites. He knocks twice.

BROOKLYN

Come!

He opens the door. The lights are out save for the corner lamps, which have thin red scarves thrown over them, casting the bedroom in a scarlet hue. Matthew steps forward, and the door shuts behind him. He turns around. There, Brooklyn poses in the same outfit as before, one hand on her hip and the other twirling her hair. She smiles, a flame-blue glint in her eyes.

MATTHEW

Brooklyn... you look—

BROOKLYN

C'mere.

She puts a finger to his lips, then inside his mouth. She then pulls it away and moves the same finger to her own and sucks on it. She places a hand on his chest and then slowly walks him back until he falls onto the bed, sprawled out.

She reaches down and undoes his belt.

MATTHEW

What are you—?

>   She tugs down at his jeans, displaying his boxer briefs.
>   She tugs on these.

MATTHEW (cont.)

Rook...

>   Matthew grabs onto the front of his underwear, keeping
>   it up. Brooklyn frowns, then straddles him on the bed.
>   She kisses him hard, hitting her teeth up against his
>   own. They kiss intensely and completely, her breath
>   hot on his face, her left hand guiding him guiding her
>   lower body. She then leans back, panting, and pulls
>   the bra forward and off with one swift motion. She
>   moves aside, and he kicks off his shoes and socks. She
>   mumbles into his ear.

BROOKLYN

I want you.

MATTHEW

(Panting.) Huh?

BROOKLYN

I said... I said *I want you*... Captain Canary.

>   Brooklyn stands, grabbing pillows and tossing them to
>   the floor. He peers up. She's lying naked on her back,

a pillow under her head and another arching her back, her body spread in a starfish fashion, wet like the sea breeze. Matthew gets down on his knees beside her. She's waiting.

He knows what she wants. Matthew can be clueless, but he's not stupid. But he doesn't want this. Her, yes, of course. Her lips, her hugs, her hands in his, but sex? Maybe later? Much, much later? What even is sex with Brooklyn? He doesn't want to swamp them both with anything like sex just yet, and he doesn't feel good anymore, his hands on her waist or anywhere, and he's not sure what she wants, what he wants, what she's doing to her or to him.

Matthew moves over to her open legs, and, as she wants, as he thinks he should want or did want at one point but not now, not really, this isn't him but it is, he positions his hands on her knees. He's never noticed these scars. He feels the one on her left leg with his thumb, but then Brooklyn rolls her eyes and reaches up and grabs his hair and pushes his head into her. She moans as he sputters. She rhythmically moves him back and forth, side to side, alternating, all in an effort to aid him in his going down on her, this cunnilingus of sorts.

He doesn't use much tongue. He tries to kiss her there, but she tastes like her fingers. It's hard for him to breathe. It's a dark place that isn't love at all—the half-light of a full moon. Remember Valentine's Day a year ago? When he'd bought her flowers, and they kept getting lost and mishandled and run over by a golf cart to the point where there was only one left? And she loved it? That was so sweet. A lot of work, but in the end, so worth it to see her smile. And she's not smiling, not anymore. He closes his eyes, and this isn't fun, and when has anything ever been fun for them since prom night, and there, now he's crying again.

That's when he realizes she's been crying too.

She lets go of his hair, and she's no longer forcing him into anything. He leans away. Brooklyn curls up and lies over onto her side, hugging one of the pillows.

Matthew eases his way up. He wipes his mouth with his sleeve, looks around, and then gathers a blanket from the bed. He gently places it over Brooklyn. She weeps some more.

BROOKLYN (cont.)

You... you didn't like that, did you?

MATTHEW

I... Rook, I wasn't...

He runs a hand over his neck. She sighs.

BROOKLYN

I'm sorry, I can't do this right now, I can't, I'm so tired. Ugh, I'm sorry. It's tough keeping everything together, being the go-to girl. I thought I had it under control... but things have gotten so out of hand. You can go, if you want. Just pack your bags and go. God knows I can't.

She stares at the wall. Matthew slowly walks over to the lamps and removes the scarves, exposing the fluorescence. Off one, he smells smoke, so he unplugs it. He turns and sees Brooklyn standing, her hands clasping the blanket around her neck and back. Matthew notices her bellybutton.

MATTHEW

You have a piercing. I forgot about that.

She kind of laughs.

BROOKLYN

Because I've only worn it once in public, and you remember all the flak I got. Same with my hair, when I went brunette that one semester. Then I dyed it back because they didn't like it.

MATTHEW

I thought it was nice.

BROOKLYN

Well... you know how it goes. Thanks.

She slips on some boy shorts and a t-shirt and socks from the floor, and then she walks over to the dresser. There, she digs around before pulling out a beige tin and setting it on the desk beside Gregg the succulent. She opens the tin and pours out a line of brown powder. She breathes it in, and her eyes surge open.

BROOKLYN (cont.)

Oh God. Bleh. Blahh.

Brooklyn wipes her nose. She smiles, then walks over next to Matthew. They sit on the floor together, against the bed, her eyes a blue emptiness.

BROOKLYN (cont.)

It's, um, cocoa snuff. Ground-up chocolate and stimulants and euphoria.

MATTHEW

You snort chocolate?

BROOKLYN

Better than an actual drug. It's no different than that coffee or Whazz we're always drinking—and Whazz paid off the FDA. It helps when you're anxious, okay? The chocolate does, I mean. It helps, the chocolate. I don't know. It's been a long past few months. So much has happened and keeps happening, and I don't want to get burned again.

MATTHEW

I don't get this. None of this, at all.

BROOKLYN

I know, and I'm sorry. We haven't been fair to you. We were so stoked to have you back, after you left for Alaska so soon. But while you were gone, things changed here, at SBA. I mean, obviously.

She eyes the pillows on the carpet.

BROOKLYN (cont.)

Down there, I thought that's what you wanted. That's what everybody thinks you boys like—we grow up believing in our one-day knight in shining armor and how we're all princesses just waiting to be a teenager so we can get a boyfriend and then figure out whatever it is these body parts are supposed to do. Until we know better, that is. But you—you're always trying to kiss me, to hold me, to touch me...

MATTHEW

I know you, Brooklyn, and I care about you. Down there, that wasn't real.

BROOKLYN

Isn't that what you want? It's what you want, right?

MATTHEW

That... wasn't you. And I'd only want to do it if it were.

BROOKLYN

You don't know me. Everyone thinks they do, but they don't. Liss, Rhys, Virgo, Fischer...

> Matthew looks at Brooklyn's right hand, her nails digging deep into her leg.

MATTHEW

Help me understand then. About you, SBA... what is this place? What is this school?

BROOKLYN

There are... a million possibilities, and the human brain can only think so deep into life. So just don't worry. It's easier.

MATTHEW

It's all I do. I worry about you, about—

BROOKLYN

And it's all Liss ever does, and it's not good for her. There are lots of reasons for living. Birds, friends, the palm trees along the sidewalk, soft orange sunsets. Being too existential can lead to horrible, horrible moods. Nobody knows what the truth is, and that's okay. It personally makes me feel a bit better when I distract myself by realizing life doesn't have to be this way. Like, maybe we, or the universe, are a computer simulation created by some higher and more intelligent beings—that's one theory. There are more ways we could be living, and it might lead to something positive, we don't know, and I think it's better that way, on this tiny moist mud ball in space. Don't burn yourself out on this. No need to be paranoid. Just focus on you and be as kind as you can. Because this... is the life that we know. Might as well take it for what it is and live it. (Nudging Matthew.) And hey, if this is some simulation, at least it means we haven't *actually* destroyed the earth as much as we have.

> Matthew smiles, remembering that one day last spring when he and the gang planted lavender and cilantro on campus to help with the declining bee population.

MATTHEW

Like that one day last spring when we planted lavender and cilantro on campus.

BROOKLYN

To help with the declining bee population—exactly. We're just doing what we're told, enjoying the life we're expected to live, the sun on our faces all year... and lately, well, yeah. Trouble in paradise. Turns out the universe might not care about us.

MATTHEW

But we care about each other.

BROOKLYN

And even if we are trapped, well, better to be trapped with someone else, right? But you have to trust me. Okay? Please.

MATTHEW

Those scars...

BROOKLYN

I dated a guy while you were away. I know, that's dumb. You and I— we spent so long not dating, and we both had this on-again, off-again thing, and when we finally wanted to try last semester, you went away, and I stupidly clung to the first pretty guy who gave me attention. And in the end, we hurt each other. But you, being here, I thought I could get past it. And I guess... I guess I can't. Maybe I'm not ready. Maybe I'm selfish. Maybe things will never change back to how they were. And maybe that's perfectly natural.

MATTHEW

I miss us, Rook.

BROOKLYN

Well... here we are. I don't know what else to tell you.

Brooklyn breathes in the filtered and recirculated

air, and she yawns, and then she rests her head on Matthew's shoulder. He yawns with her. He wishes this moment could last forever, hovering in a dark nebula.

BROOKLYN (cont.)

Do you remember the day we met?

Matthew laughs.

MATTHEW

That fountain was refreshing.

BROOKLYN

I meant that night, under the stars. That was nice. You and me.

MATTHEW

Seems like a lifetime ago.

BROOKLYN

We were kids.

MATTHEW

Are we not?

Brooklyn doesn't answer, and Matthew can't blame her for it. They close their eyes together as the air conditioning hums softly above them. It's soothing in a way. Familiar. They sit like this for hours.

A bird's eye view of Sea Breeze Academy at night, shimmering in the moonlight, and then the credits roll.

1. Hey Darren, you heating up on E-10s? Or are they still closed?
2. Nah we're just holding at these temperatures until they're ready to start up. Leaving them closed till then.
1. OK.

"WELCOME TO SBA: PART 2"

Brooklyn and her new roommates go to the dean's mansion for the annual back-to-school festivities.

A nother perfect day in Southern California. Outside Room 102 in Dutton Suites, Brooklyn stands in a red beaded party dress, waiting. She knocks on the door.

BROOKLYN

Almost done?

VIRGO

Almost!

Brooklyn shakes her head, though she's smiling all the same. She walks over to a poster on the wall. *Celebrate the new year at the dean's open house*, it reads. *Eat, meet new people, and have a great time at our annual Winter Fiesta-val! Shuttles leave the G. M. Jenkins Administration Offices at seven o'clock. Ask your dorm advisor for more information.*

The door opens to reveal Virgo in a little navy

dress with a cutout back and a flattering fit. Her hair is fitted with several small decorative braids tied off with feathers. She strikes a pose.

BROOKLYN

Wow, you look great!

VIRGO

Aww shucks. Makin' me blush. But first! The bathroom. B-R-B.

Virgo hurries down the hall. She passes Liss Williams, a small black girl with straightened hair and glasses who's fast-walking away from Sage.

SAGE

Liss! Liss! Please reconsider!

LISS WILLIAMS

I'm not a people-person!

SAGE

You don't know that!

Sage stops in front of Brooklyn.

SAGE (cont.)

Hey, Brooklyn, would you mind talking with Liss? She's a resident here like yourself. She's less into hanging out with people and more into... well, experimenting on them.

BROOKLYN

Experimenting?

SAGE

She's a science prodigy—extremely gifted—but she doesn't have many friends, so she rarely leaves her room. I think going to the festivities tonight would do her some good. Would you be her buddy for the evening? Please?

BROOKLYN

Uh, sure, yeah, of course.

SAGE

Oh, thank you. I worry about her, but there's so much work I need to do here before classes start up again. Anyway, I'm off to go count money. Enjoy the dean's house tonight!

BROOKLYN

Thanks! Will do!

> Sage exits. Brooklyn walks down the hall to where Liss is standing outside an open door, measuring its frame.

BROOKLYN (cont.)

Hey there. Liss, right? I'm Brooklyn.

LISS

(Measuring.) What do you think of the number seven hundred and eighty-four thousand, six hundred and thirty-one? No arguing.

BROOKLYN

I, umm, I think, it's big? (Beat.) I've never counted that high.

LISS

It's interesting. Seven plus eight is fifteen, four plus six is ten, and three plus one is four. Then fifteen plus ten is twenty-five, twenty-five plus four is twenty-nine, and two plus nine is eleven. Two ones. Upside down, it spells I-E-P-H-B-L, which could potentially be an acronym for "Is Edmund Possibly Halting Baggage to London?" But it could also be a car plate, or a zip code in Corpus Christi if you drop the one. Of course it's divisible by itself, but seventy-eight minus forty-six minus thirty-one is, unsurprisingly, one. By itself. Alone. Just some sort of forgotten data in the mass cyberspace world. (Beat.) Fair warning though: my answer has not been checked for rounding errors, quantization errors, signal noise, or quantum fluctuations.

Brooklyn stares at Liss, then blinks.

BROOKLYN

Wow, okay, so, also, did you hear about the party tonight at the dean's house?

Liss stretches her arms above her head.

LISS

I got the invitation, but I have no clue why. The email says there will be free food, drinks, and many other things, but nowhere does it mention rats are allowed. So I must decline.

BROOKLYN

You... have rats.

LISS

Off the books, yes. Besides, I'd feel guilty eating without my rats. I would just be awkwardly standing alone in the corner, stuffing my face with whatever sweets are available.

BROOKLYN

It could be fun though, meeting new people, talking, exchanging contact info—

LISS

That's what lawyers do. Lawyers freak me out. Besides, I wouldn't know anyone.

BROOKLYN

Well, you'd know me, and I like sweets as much as the next girl. I'll stuff my face in the corner with you!

> Liss narrows her eyes, studying Brooklyn. Then she relaxes and laughs.

LISS

You'd do that for me?

BROOKLYN

Sure! (Nudging Liss.) Plus I hear there might be churros.

LISS

My favorite Spanish fried-dough pastry!

BROOKLYN

Great! Think you can be ready in ten?

LISS

Sure. Just let me see if the door's big enough for Rob.

BROOKLYN

Who?

LISS

Rob Otto. He's, like, my best friend.

> Liss pockets her measuring tape and takes out a remote. She presses the red button.
>
> The doorframe collapses as a large and bulky robot bursts through the wall. It has three green eye lights, an engine above its torso, and pinchers for hands. Brooklyn screams. Rob Otto screams, albeit mechanically.

LISS (cont.)

Stop it, you'll scare him!

BROOKLYN

What is that?!

LISS

The reason my tuition is low and insurance is high…

ROB OTTO

Scanning area. Foreign lifeform detected.

> Rob Otto's eyes turn red. Liss stands between him and
> Brooklyn.

LISS

Rob, Rob, *Robert*, this is Brooklyn, my... (Smiling.) My new friend.
She's a good one.

> Rob Otto's eyes relax to green.

BROOKLYN

What happens to the bad ones?!

> Smoke emits from Rob Otto's engine.

ROB OTTO

Critical error. Overheating.

LISS

Uh-oh.

> Liss guides Rob Otto back into the room.

LISS (cont.)

Ummm, so, meet you by the shuttles in ten!

BROOKLYN

Yeah—yeah, t-t-totally!

ROB OTTO

I only wanted to be loved.

> Brooklyn, alone again, puts a hand to her head. She then turns around to see Miki in strappy heels and a black cold-shoulder shimmer dress with short sleeves. Her hair is in a French twist. Miki glances over to the hole in the wall. She nods knowingly.

MIKI

Ah, you met Liss Williams. She means well. Almost blew up the school once or twice, so yeah, she's a goober, but well-intentioned. Anyway, you ready?

BROOKLYN

I told Liss I'd wait for her by the shuttles.

MIKI

Then let's bounce! We'll save her a seat.

> Brooklyn and Miki stop by the restrooms to meet up with Virgo, and then the three walk the way to the administration offices, where students are loading onto shuttles. Liss turns up soon after in a sky-blue top, white skater-style skirt, and matching canvas sneakers. Together, the four girls enter one of the shuttles. From the pink clouds to the glowing red of the sunset over the ocean, it's clear that Brooklyn and her new friends are in for a beautiful night, and also, that it's time for a commercial.

* * *

Back at Sea Breeze Academy, Brooklyn, Miki, Virgo, and Liss have arrived at Dean Fischer's immaculate mansion to the south of campus. The front contains an entryway, porte cochere, and multiple fountains. The Gothic-Tudor style is accentuated by the full moon shining bright over the Pacific Ocean, creating a stunning, shimmering backdrop. Brooklyn looks around in awe as she passes through the entrance and into the lush green grass.

BROOKLYN

Holy cow...

MIKI

"Santa vaca," more like. It's a fiesta! Where's your spirit?

VIRGO

My spirit's in wherever they have the food set up. You saw the email— all you can eat!

The girls walk into the courtyard, which features an outdoor kitchen, a barbeque area, and a large, colorful koi pond with an artificial stream, the big fish mindlessly swimming in circles. Beyond the terrace is a small citrus orchard, and from the ground, blue and pink lights beam onto the mansion's exterior walls. A Mariachi band plays in the back, and some students are already dancing in a conga line. Lanterns hang

above the dance floor. The nearby patio is decorated
with orange streamers, matching piñatas, potted cacti,
and tables of chips, salsa, churros, nachos, sodas, and
bottles of sparkling grape juice.

MIKI

Oh gross. Rhys is wearing so much cologne, you can just about taste
him twenty feet away.

VIRGO

Yuck.

Rhys stands in line at the do-it-yourself taco bar by the
swimming pool grotto. He's wearing a tailored three-
piece suit, and he keeps pouring too much sour cream
onto his taco and having to scrape it to the side in
frustration. He stands separate from everyone else.

VIRGO (cont.)

Poor guy. I almost feel sorry for him.

MIKI

Almost.

LISS

He called me a basket case once…

BROOKLYN

Who is he? I bumped into him earlier today. He got, like, unreasonably
mad.

MIKI

That's Rhys Underwood. His mom's in the industry, which is the only reason he gets to attend SBA—because he's loaded. His grades are awful, he's average at sports, and he cheated on his internal assessment for psychology last semester. Him and his wrestling buddies. They reused old experiment data from some dude's brother who graduated, and of course they were caught because the profs at Jepperson Hall keep everything on record. What did they expect? The boys were expelled for plagiarism, but Rhys got off the hook because his mother donates thousands to the school every year. It's pretty lame. Everyone knows he cheated, the goober. But hey, maybe this is a better punishment for him—being a pariah, a social outcast, a *persona non grata*.

VIRGO

Olé!

       Miki spies the food tables.

MIKI

There are those churros. Come to momma.

       They walk over. Miki opens her large purse and casually
       stuffs handfuls of churros inside.

MIKI (cont.)

Churros are cheaper than therapy. Hey, Virgo, what even is a churro?

VIRGO

How would I know?

MIKI

Well, you know… I'm from Canada, you're from…?

VIRGO

Fresno?

MIKI

Okay.

> Miki picks up multiple sodas.

MIKI (cont.)

Well, I'm going to take these and socialize. I probably won't remember anything in the morning, so see you all later!

BROOKLYN

(Laughing.) Bye!

VIRGO

Later, skater. (To Brooklyn and Liss.) Hey, let's go inside. I want to see the house.

LISS

Are we allowed to bring in food?

VIRGO

Pssh, with my tuition, we'd better!

> Virgo stuffs a plate with enchiladas while Brooklyn pours herself a cup of water. They take them inside

the dean's house, which is decorated for the event with multicolored blankets hanging on the walls, as well as terracotta vases, pitchers, and pots. Floor-to-ceiling windows show off the party outside. Chris, in a white accent sports coat, sees Brooklyn from across the elegant main living room. He approaches the girls.

CHRIS

Hey, Oklahomie. Hey, Virgo. 'Sup, Liss.

LISS

Word up, my dude! This party's poppin' and sizzling, yo!

Brooklyn, Virgo, and Chris stare at Liss. She looks away.

LISS (cont.)

Sorry. I mostly talk to robots and strangers online.

CHRIS

And what do they say…?

LISS

Not much. Usually they just ask about my first pet, the street I grew up on, and my mother's maiden name.

BROOKLYN

I would change my passwords if I were you.

LISS

On it.

Liss whips out her cell phone and starts pressing buttons. She walks elsewhere, her framed face focused on the screen.

CHRIS

So Virgo, are you still hosting your book club this semester?

VIRGO

You know it! Larger emphasis on plays this time around. I'm thinking we'll start with *Hamlet*, or maybe *Agamemnon*.

CHRIS

Ah, yes, the dark return of the king from his victories at war. "Even in our sleep, pain, which cannot forget, falls drop by drop upon the heart until, in our own despair, against our will, comes wisdom through the awful grace of God."

Virgo leans over to Brooklyn.

VIRGO

He's quoting Aeschylus. "By suffering comes wisdom!"

CHRIS

I'll tell Matthew that I saw you, Brooklyn. He was looking for you earlier.

VIRGO

Who, Matthew Flynn?

BROOKLYN

Looking for me?

CHRIS

Oh. (Beat.) I probably shouldn't have said that.

> Denzel Davis, a handsome black guy in a tuxedo, walks into the room. Chris waves him over.

CHRIS (cont.)

Hey, brother, what's up!

> They fist-bump.

DENZEL DAVIS

Nothing much, nothing much.

VIRGO

Omigosh, omigosh, Denzel Davis, aaaaahh!

DENZEL

Virgo! Good to see you again.

> Virgo, grinning wide, embraces Denzel. He stumbles back a bit, then accepts, smiling. Brooklyn waits as Virgo lets go of him.

BROOKLYN

You… look familiar. Do I know you from somewhere?

DENZEL

Oh, right. I'm number nine on the FBI's Most Wanted list. Don't tell anybody.

CHRIS

Man, don't scare the girl!

Chris turns to Brooklyn.

CHRIS (cont.)

He's the *SBA News* reporter I was telling you about. This is Denzel Davis. You might've seen him on one of the TVs.

Denzel extends a hand.

DENZEL

Pleasure to meet you.

Brooklyn takes it and shakes it.

BROOKLYN

Likewise.

DENZEL

Well, I have to go cover this speech the dean's about to make. I'll see you three outside.

CHRIS

Later, bro.

The music is louder now. As Brooklyn turns to face it, she accidentally bumps into a suited white-faced man with thinning hair, spilling her cup onto his jacket. This is Dean Charles Fischer.

BROOKLYN

Oh my God, sir, professor man, I am so sorry—

Virgo steps in between them.

VIRGO

Oh, Dean Fischer, why hello there! Lovely home you have here!

BROOKLYN

It's just water, if it helps...

Dean Fischer puts up a hand.

DEAN CHARLES FISCHER

No worries. It's all right, girls. Accidents happen.

The dean takes off his blazer and places it over one of the nearby chairs. He smiles back at them.

DEAN FISCHER (cont.)

Virgo, nice to see you. Great job in *The Rocky Horror Show*. And Chris, excellent flute work during last season's music festival. I'm surprised you didn't play on the court again this year, but the SBA band is lucky to have you.

CHRIS

Hey, thanks, Dean-o!

Dean Fischer crosses his arms.

DEAN FISCHER

Too casual.

Chris nods. The dean faces Brooklyn.

DEAN FISCHER (cont.)

I'm sorry, I don't think we've met.

BROOKLYN

Hi, uh, Brooklyn Rivers.

VIRGO

She's a transfer from Oklahoma.

Dean Fischer laughs.

DEAN FISCHER

Oklahoma. Watch out for twisters!

The kids stare blankly at him.

CHRIS

Twister? Is that a dance move?

VIRGO

An adult beverage?

BROOKLYN

(Shaking her head.) No, he means a tornado.

VIRGO

Ohhh, okay.

CHRIS

Gotcha.

DEAN FISCHER

Anyway, time for me to address your classmates. I want to make our Hispanic students feel right at home.

> Brooklyn, Virgo, and Chris walk with him across the mansion and toward the back doors.

VIRGO

How do you do it, Dean Fischer? Talking to a crowd this big, I mean. I've done school productions, but those are nowhere near this size.

> The dean shrugs.

DEAN FISCHER

Oh, it's easy up there. I just imagine them in their underwear.

> The audience, mostly teenagers, stands before the raised patio stage, eagerly awaiting the dean. Brooklyn, Virgo, and Chris join the gathering. They all applaud as Dean Fischer walks out to the microphone.

DEAN FISCHER (cont.)

Thank you, thank you! And thank you to the Academy. It's great to be here at this casa fiesta with you all tonight, celebrating another semester at SBA, our home away from home.

The audience claps to this.

DEAN FISCHER (cont.)

I will keep this brief, as I know you're all out having fun here before classes start this next week. It's true we are a boarding school founded on the belief in scholarship, good grades, and study habits. But we're also focused on student autonomy, on reflection, on *personal engagement*. So yes, cut out distractions and do well this semester, but also take the time to invest in friends. Positive connections with people are vital to our happiness, and even then, we must strive beyond the simplest solution. Going to school for the purpose of schooling is not necessarily bad thinking—it's what your parents are paying for! But… it's going into a garden and stopping at a rosebush, and being satisfied with the rosebush, when beyond that is a cemetery, a pool, and so much left to explore. So talk to people. Go out on Friday nights, see a movie on campus, make friends as you navigate the fires of youth. And if you're unhappy with the way you present yourself, don't feel confined to it. Now is as good a time as any to explore who you are as an individual. There are too many people to try to impress, so why bother? Definitely take care of yourself and wear nice clothes and brush your hair—be impressive that way—but don't try to do everything at once. It will tear you down, and it'll do it real quick. So go on. Enjoy this next semester. School is tough, but so are you. And don't you ever forget that. *Make waves!*

AUDIENCE

Make waves!

DEAN FISCHER

Excellent. Now let's ándale over to the party, dance away the winter blues, and have a maraca-shaking good time!

> The crowd applauds. The dean exits the stage, and the students depart for the party.
>
> Miki waltzes into Brooklyn. Miki is stumbling around and giggling, and her soda sloshes around in her cup.

MIKI

Brooklyn! Oh, Brooklyn, good, you're here. So... so good you're here, with us... at SBA!

BROOKLYN

I... agree!

MIKI

Where... where's Virgo?

VIRGO

Right here.

MIKI

Great! Let's make it a threesome. 'Cause we, heh, we have to decide who's on kitchen duty this week, remember?

> Virgo grins next to Miki.

VIRGO

Oh, that's right, that's right. Brooklyn doesn't know about our little tradition.

BROOKLYN

Should I be scared?

MIKI

Nah. We're not gonna make you steal food from the cafeteria or chug a soft drink. We have something a little more... a little more fun in mind.

> Five or so other girls gather around Miki, Virgo, and Brooklyn.

MIKI (cont.)

It's a game we call "Vampire." (Playfully sneering.) You have to bite the neck of a cute guy you like before the night's over.

BROOKLYN

Cute guys are so overrated.

MIKI

Sure, but the last girl gets kitchen duty—and trust me, during the first week when everyone's trying out their new recipes with all the free time they have, you do *not* want kitchen duty.

BROOKLYN

What about Liss?

MIKI

If that's what you're into…

BROOKLYN

Like, is she participating?

VIRGO

Ohhh no. Ask that girl to wipe down the counters and she sics Rob Otto on you. And his eyes turn red! All three of 'em!

MIKI

Any other questions, ladies? No? All right! Find someone who treats you like SBA treats the lawn!

VIRGO

Wait, no, I'm still eating!

MIKI

Vámanos, Virgo! Vámanos! Last one back's a freakish goober!

Miki, Virgo, and the girls all run off in different directions, leaving Brooklyn panicked and confused.

The mariachi music grows louder, more dramatic. Grounds workers parade around with boxes of complementary maracas and large sombreros. Brooklyn darts left and looks all over. There's a guy standing alone—but there's his girlfriend, bringing him a cup of whatever. Brooklyn darts right. There, by the tree, another guy! No, he's being led by the hand by someone else.

The conga line sweeps Brooklyn into the crowd of dancers. Everything is dark except for brief bursts of neon pink and blue. She catches a glimpse of Miki biting down on a dude's neck. No, not one dude—two, three? She can't even tell. Miki's laughing.

Brooklyn stands on her tiptoes, leans forward, trips on her own two feet, and then falls onto Matthew. She grabs onto his shoulders for support—as he grabs ahold of her—and then she positions her mouth on his neck and, with an apologetic expression, sucks at his skin for a sudden second.

She pulls away, sending Matthew backward into the grass. He's flustered and wearing a suit a bit too big for him. Brooklyn wipes the saliva off her lips as she leaves, too embarrassed with herself to look back. From the enamored look on his face, it's clear that Matthew has fallen in love this evening, and also, that it's time for a commercial.

* * *

Back at Sea Breeze Academy, Brooklyn, on the verge of tears, runs away from the dance floor. The nighttime sky is a dark blue, and the moon is full and spirited. Distracted, Brooklyn stumbles forward into none other than Rhys. He turns around, disoriented, and then scowls at her.

RHYS

What, you think you can just keep running me over like that?!

BROOKLYN

I'm sorry—

        He walks away.

RHYS

Whatever.

BROOKLYN

I said I'm sorry! Okay?! *I'm sorry!*

        He stops and turns around.

RHYS

Hey... you okay?

BROOKLYN

Yes! (Beat.) No.

        Brooklyn sits in a chair facing the lit pool. It's filled
        with crystal, sky-blue water, sparkling and twirling
        with the stars above. Rhys eases his way down beside
        her. He puts his hands in his pockets.

RHYS

Oh gosh. Okay. Umm... so, yelling at you earlier, that was... my bad.
I shouldn't have.

BROOKLYN

(Wiping a tear from her eye.) Yeah. Well. A lot's been going on.

RHYS

You're new, right?

Brooklyn, staring at the water, nods.

RHYS (cont.)

Right. This'll be my eighth semester at SBA. Started in sixth grade, and here I am. 'Cept all my friends are gone now. So I'm... alone, I guess.

BROOKLYN

I'd heard you'd plagiarized with your teammates, and they got expelled.

RHYS

What? That's—no, I didn't... cheat. No. I follow the rules—I do! I... well, it doesn't look good for me either way. (Shaking his head.) Dean Fischer talks about *reinventing ourselves* or whatever, as if. You, well, you can do that, sure, no one knows you. But me? Not that simple.

BROOKLYN

It's not that easy for me either. New school, new classes, new people. It's weird. Different. I'm not used to this. Everything's a little... a little faster here. I can tell that already. And everyone's nice, of course, but that doesn't mean they know that I don't live in a teepee where I'm from, or that we don't ride horses to the saloons, or they don't know what a twister is—

RHYS

A twist... what?

BROOKLYN

Tornado. The ground spirals of wind.

> Brooklyn imitates this with her fingers. Rhys nods.

RHYS

For me, it literally feels like a tornado's been through this campus. I don't recognize it at all.

BROOKLYN

You mean "figuratively." Or else the school would be destroyed from all the debris.

RHYS

Pssh, wow, okay, Grammar Girl.

> Brooklyn laughs. Behind her and Rhys is Matthew, walking around. When he spies the two, he jumps in alarm and quickly hides behind a rosebush.

RHYS (cont.)

Say, maybe after classes this week, me and you could go to Fukutsū, the sushi place in Mintz Plaza. You know, just for the halibut. (Beat.) Or on a date.

> Brooklyn smiles.

BROOKLYN

Thanks, but I'm not really interested in dating right now, so soon.

RHYS

I... I didn't cheat, you know.

BROOKLYN

I believe you. Still, I just got here. I miss my mom, my dogs, the apple tree in my yard back home... It's a whirlwind of emotions. I need to find my way first.

She stands.

BROOKLYN (cont.)

We should hang out though. You, me, your roommates, mine. And Liss Williams. I'll vouch for you. You can explain it to them like you did to me.

RHYS

Liss though? I dunno. She's kind of freaky. Doesn't she have a robot?

BROOKLYN

(Smiling.) She means well.

Rhys stands with her. He looks around.

RHYS

I'm gonna grab a soda. You want one?

BROOKLYN

No, but thank you. I think I'll stay here a bit. Reflect.

RHYS

Oh, I get it, because of the water. Like, your reflection.

Brooklyn laughs.

BROOKLYN

I'll see you around.

She gives him a catch-you-later nod, and he walks away. Brooklyn looks down at the pool and then takes off her flats and sits at the edge, dipping her feet in. She listens to the croaking of the frogs and the buzzing of the insects. She sighs.

A rustling from the bushes. Matthew tumbles out and rolls into the grass and then catches his balance and leaps to his feet. He sees Brooklyn. Brooklyn sees him. She gives Matthew a small smile. He walks over and squats beside her.

BROOKLYN (cont.)

Hey. Sorry about that before. Your neck. There's this thing with the girls—some kind of party game to avoid kitchen duty, I'm not sure. That was dumb of me. I'm sorry.

MATTHEW

Hey, no, you're totally fine, totally... fine. Seriously. You gotta do whatcha gotta do, right?

BROOKLYN

Sure. Something like that.

> Matthew takes off his shoes and socks and then rolls up his pant legs. He dangles his feet in the water with her.

MATTHEW

So… did you meet your roommates yet? (Cringing.) I mean, of course you have—uh, what are they like? Are they nice?

BROOKLYN

Yeah, they are. Miki Mizushima and Virgo Torres. Well, Virgo's her nickname. I forget her actual name.

MATTHEW

Oh yeah, I know them, they're cool. (Beat.) Coolio, they are.

> Brooklyn pulls her feet out and turns to face Matthew. She crosses her legs.

BROOKLYN

So I feel bad about your *Captain Canary* comic book.

MATTHEW

Don't, really. I told you, it's no problem at all—

BROOKLYN

But it got me thinking. If you had to be half a bird, would you rather it be your top half or bottom half?

Matthew laughs.

MATTHEW

Well, I... need more details. What kind of bird? What's my habitat? Which half gets the wings? If I choose top, do I keep my human brain? (Sighing.) With my luck, I'd pick top and get a flightless bird.

BROOKLYN

I think I'd choose the top 'cause I think it'd be funny to not be able to communicate in any language known to humans. (Beat.) Actually, no. I'd choose bottom because I assume the bottom half would be subject to bird-levels of modesty and I'd never have to wear pants.

MATTHEW

You do realize how strange it would look to have a woman's head and upper torso on a bird's legs, right?

Brooklyn raises an eyebrow.

BROOKLYN

You saying I couldn't pull it off?

MATTHEW

Oh, well, no, that's not, uh, that's not what I'm—

BROOKLYN

If centaurs can make it work, why not me, right? (Laughing.) Don't overthink it. Life is full of hard questions. What will be... what could have been... what would be better... a bird upper body or a bird lower body?

MATTHEW

Ummm, neither? Both are equally awful.

BROOKLYN

Yes, it's a ridiculous scenario and both options are bad. The fun is in choosing which to live with. (Nudging him.) And hey—maybe if you had a bird upper body, your bird brain could help you forget the *apparent pain* of having to choose.

Matthew grins.

MATTHEW

Fine. I pick... left-side bird, right-side human.

Brooklyn laughs again.

BROOKLYN

Lame. Do bottom-half bird. Then you'd get some sick talons. That's what I'd pick at least. I'd be a bird, you know? Wearing no pants means I could mess up a *lot* of cars.

MATTHEW

I mean, you can mess up a lot of cars now. Pants aren't stopping you.

She smiles. He smiles with her.

BROOKLYN

Whatever, birdbrain.

MATTHEW

Whatever, Rook.

BROOKLYN

Rook?

MATTHEW

Short for rookie! You still got some ways to go before you're a master of this campus like myself.

BROOKLYN

So I can trust you'll show me all the cool, secret spots, right?

MATTHEW

Oh, definitely.

BROOKLYN

Ha. Coolio.

> They smile together. Suddenly, Miki, Virgo, Chris, Liss, and Rhys walk over by the pool area, see Brooklyn and Matthew, and then make their way over to them. Miki's bumbling here and there with her refilled cup of soda, and Virgo carries her plate of tacos over her head as she maneuvers around the pool. Rhys drinks from his own cup. They all look happy.

BROOKLYN (cont.)

Hey, guys.

VIRGO

Brooklyn, Brooklyn! Look what Miki got you!

> Virgo sets her plate on one of the chairs and takes out her cell phone. She shows the screen to Brooklyn.

VIRGO (cont.)

Miki took that photograph you brought, and with Sage's help, we made it bigger, and ta-da! A giant print for your wall!

> Sure enough, the picture on the phone is of Brooklyn's side of their dorm room. The Oklahoma sunset is now a poster hanging over her bed, the original propped up against a pillow. Brooklyn smiles wide, her eyes full of tears. She hugs Virgo, then pulls Miki in with them.

BROOKLYN

You guys are amazing. Thank you so, so much. I love it!

MIKI

Hey, we roommates gotta look out for each other.

> Chris looks first to Rhys, then Matthew.

CHRIS

That's right, fellas. We're all in it together.

RHYS

Might as well make the most of it.

Liss takes an empty cup and fills it with pool water. The others follow suit.

LISS

(Raising her cup.) To Brooklyn.

MATTHEW

To Rook!

VIRGO

To Rook!

BROOKLYN

To Sea Breeze Academy!

CHRIS

Make waves!

RHYS

Make waves!

MIKI

Here, here!

The gang pours their cups of water back into the pool, "Auld Lang Syne" playing in the background, sweet and hopeful. They laugh, and they smile, and they are unmistakably glad to be there, all of them, together. Matthew tries to balance a cup on his head, and when the water spills down his face, Liss tries too. Chris and

Brooklyn toss tortilla chips to try to knock the cups off. Miki, Rhys, and Virgo lounge about, watching and cheering on their friends.

A bird's eye view of the sparkling campus at night, and then the credits roll.

1. Hey Arty, I'm looking at bringing this up to 200 degrees now.
2. What's that, Mike?
1. Procedure calls for 200 degrees.
2. OK. 200 degrees.

"MERRY CHRISTMAS, MATTHEW"

Upset after realizing the gang has never celebrated Christmas together, Brooklyn organizes a Yuletide celebration for her friends.

Another perfect day in Southern California. Matthew, Virgo, Rhys, and Chris, still wearing that eyepatch, are taking it easy in the girls' lounge at Dutton Suites. On the TV is an episode of *Squawky!*, a cartoon about a teenage boy in a bird costume who gets adopted from the pet store by an oblivious couple, to the annoyance of their own teenage son. The show follows the son's endeavors to expose Squawky as a human boy. It's funny because everybody's ignorant.

RHYS

Want some oranges?

> Rhys holds up a bowl of clementines. Virgo shrugs.

VIRGO

Oh, sure, what the heck.

Virgo, Chris, and Rhys each take an orange from the bowl. They then jab their thumbs repeatedly into their oranges until a dent appears before they proceed to tear off the skin in approximately three-to-four million individual pieces. After, they put the orange segments onto plates and eat directly off the plates like dogs because their fingers are too covered in orange to pick anything up anymore. They then clean everything within a two-feet radius, including their clothing, because it's now all covered in orange juice. Naturally.

Meanwhile, Matthew's been staring out one of the windows.

MATTHEW

Guys, there are some... some donkeys outside? And one's nibbling the grass in the shade?

VIRGO

Yeah, I see, like, five of them every day. They're pretty cute. Did you know they hurt more people than sharks do on a yearly basis?

CHRIS

Falling coconuts do as well.

RHYS

Is that a fact?

VIRGO

People are around donkeys a lot more than they are around sharks.

CHRIS

Same with coconuts.

VIRGO

Pssh, *coconuts*. In this economy?

> Matthew returns to the couches. He sits with Virgo, Chris, and Rhys. He hears something—a song that he recognizes. Matthew looks up.

MATTHEW

Is that... music playing?

RHYS

Do you see music? Does looking up help you see the music?

VIRGO

Should we call Nurse Morgan?

RHYS

Send you to the wacky shack?

> Brooklyn enters the room wearing a red-and-green-striped scarf, reindeer antlers, and carrying a bell. She rings it, smiling. The music is now distinctly a medley of "Deck the Halls" and "O Christmas Tree."

BROOKLYN

Why does Santa have three gardens?

MATTHEW

Brooklyn, what—?

BROOKLYN

So he can hoe hoe hoe!

> She rings the bell again. Virgo, Chris, and Rhys all grin.

RHYS

But the holidays ended months ago!

BROOKLYN

Sure, during winter break. But you know what I've realized? We've never celebrated Christmas together here at SBA!

> Virgo, Chris, and Rhys shift uncomfortably in their seats.

VIRGO

But Brooklyn... Christmas is a... a *religious* holiday.

BROOKLYN

No, I'm talking about *American* Christmas. The secular season. With tree trimming and giving presents and going door to door singing and putting up lots of shiny red and green baubles and Santa and his elves and *consumerism!*

> Virgo, Chris, and Rhys smile once more. Brooklyn sits with them.

VIRGO

I *adore* Christmas wearables—they're, like, a permanent fixture in my closet. I love the aesthetics of Christmas and its inherent nostalgia.

Matthew scratches his head.

MATTHEW

So you're wanting Christmas in May? (Laughing to himself.) Has it always been this warm in December?

BROOKLYN

No, I'm wanting Christmas *at SBA*. I already got it approved by Dean Fischer. My uncle in Oklahoma works at a Christmasland—like, one of those year-round holiday stores. Anyway, I emailed him about how sad I was that I've never gotten to spend Christmas with my friends, and so he sent a bunch of decorations for us to use!

Chris leans back, his hands behind his head.

CHRIS

Ah, yes. That one convenient uncle in every family.

VIRGO

It's true we've never celebrated the holidays together, especially being here in SoCal, where it's always so hot and there's never any snow. It'd be fun to hang some ornaments—

MATTHEW

But! But no mistletoe, right? It would...

The others impatiently wait for him to finish. Matthew gulps.

MATTHEW (cont.)

'Cause it promotes sexual assault?

VIRGO

Not really, no.

RHYS

Grinch.

MATTHEW

But—

VIRGO

We could dress in ugly sweaters, go sledding, have an old man hired to be Santa just to keep up the conspiracy, sing some carols—

CHRIS

Oh, I know a Carol.

RHYS

I know a Carolyn.

BROOKLYN

Caroling? Yeah, we can go caroling if you like. And hey—if we're underwater?

She rings the bell.

BROOKLYN (cont.)

We'll sing some *corals!*

> Virgo, Chris, and Rhys groan.

BROOKLYN (cont.)

And we totally have to make each other presents.

RHYS

Pssh. I got this. I am the king of Christmas gifts.

BROOKLYN

But you can't buy ours, Rhys. That's the only rule. It has to come from the heart!

RHYS

What?! No fair!

MATTHEW

Your heart is a muscle. You should exercise it.

RHYS

Nooooo, the goodness, my heart… it burns…

CHRIS

Ha. Try pickle juice then. (Beat.) Nevermind.

MATTHEW

Brooklyn, you said you want to celebrate Christmas with your friends, right? Well, kind of hard to bring the holiday cheer to *all* your friends without Liss here, right?

RHYS

What do you mean?

VIRGO

Matthew, she's over there in the corner.

> They point to "Liss" sitting by herself. "Liss" slouches.

MATTHEW

You guys, I know that isn't Liss.

> "Liss" is actually twelve Rottweiler puppies in a trench coat with a hat. Brooklyn rings the bell again and they scamper off merrily.

VIRGO

(Laughing.) Oh gosh! So random!

RHYS

Look at Matthew. I almost feel bad for him—losing his mind at such a young age.

MATTHEW

Don't underestimate me.

RHYS

Ooooh, something revolutionary and controversial. There, I said it for you. You're welcome.

BROOKLYN

Liss transferred to Aruba, remember?

CHRIS

Which is odd, considering summer's in a couple of weeks.

RHYS

Well, she was a weirdo.

CHRIS

Dude.

RHYS

Go then! See if it's everything you dreamed of!

                  Chris rolls his eyes. Rhys shrugs.

CHRIS

Tina left too.

VIRGO

Shame. I liked her.

MATTHEW

Oh come on! I bet you don't even know her last name!

VIRGO

Sure I do! (Beat.) Fox.

BROOKLYN

Warner.

RHYS

Paramount.

They look to Chris.

CHRIS

Yes, Foxwarnerparamount. That is correct.

BROOKLYN

It's Christmas, y'all! Be of good cheer! Be jolly! It's a wonderful life!

VIRGO

Yes! I call making the hot cocoa! (Leaning in to whisper to Matthew.) The key is a splash of tropical colada. Miki taught me that.

Chris turns to face Rhys.

CHRIS

Well, man, I guess we're off to find some—I mean, *make some*—Christmas gifts.

RHYS

Cool. Let's stop by our dorm first. I wanna pick up some earplugs.

CHRIS

What for?

Brooklyn rings the bell again. Rhys covers his ears and groans.

Rhys and Virgo stand, stretch, and then exit through the main doors. Brooklyn turns to leave as well, but Matthew grabs her by the shoulder.

MATTHEW

Brooklyn. Liss was twelve puppies.

She pushes him off.

BROOKLYN

Yeah, and the sky is an artificial blue. What's your point?

MATTHEW

I'm not comfortable with this! With how—with the way things have been happening! With you, with me, with our friends and Pulov from Yuran and then Miki, who's apparently been living under the school this entire time?! It's like we're collectively losing our minds here! *Or maybe it's just me!*

Chris looks away, shielding his one eye from the drama. Brooklyn sighs, then places her fingers on Matthew's shoulders, massaging him.

BROOKLYN

Relax. *Relax*. All right?

MATTHEW

No, not all right!

BROOKLYN

Breathe. In through the nose, out through the mouth. Drink some eggnog and fa-la-la-la-la. Okay? You said you'd trust me. (Tilting her head.) Are you seeing things? Getting enough sleep?

MATTHEW

No! I mean, yes! I'm not crazy!

CHRIS

Man, you just don't know when to quit.

BROOKLYN

No matter the cost to others around him.

MATTHEW

What?!

BROOKLYN

Shut up.

MATTHEW

Brooklyn!

BROOKLYN

Shut up or I die. Either that, or I'll kill you first.

MATTHEW

No.

BROOKLYN

Yes. They say if you fall and die in a dream, you die in real life. Which would be better? I die, or I kill you.

MATTHEW

You want me to act like nothing ever happened, but I'm sorry, I *can't* do that!

BROOKLYN

You are going to get yourself killed!

> They stop. No one breathes. Brooklyn looks around, then settles again on Matthew. She forces a smile.

BROOKLYN (cont.)

Remember that play I wrote? Two years ago? The one you starred in? Pretend this is a play, or whatever, and you're an actor. Your role is the adorable white nice-guy deuteragonist. Got it, birdbrain? Now perk up. Be an actor! *Enjoy the show.*

> Brooklyn ruffles his hair before exiting. Matthew looks wearily to Chris, who merely shrugs in reply to the absurdity.

CHRIS

Man... sit down for a sec.

> Matthew hesitates, then sits in one of the chairs. Chris pulls another up close to him and sits across from Matthew.

CHRIS (cont.)

You were gone for almost a whole season.

MATTHEW

The spring, right, so what? It doesn't matter. I'm done! I've had it! This is crazy, you all are crazy and formulaic and, no offense, *weird*, with your platitudes and your euphemisms and whatnot, and... and I'm ticked off, and I'm leaving!

CHRIS

What?! Leaving?! Where?

MATTHEW

This freakish school—Sea Breeze Academy! If you can even call this a school! When was the last time you went to all seven of your classes, huh? Do you even remember a day?! Liss knew! She had it all figured out! And now she's gone, just like Pulov!

CHRIS

Dude, bro, calm down, please. We can go to the beach—

MATTHEW

No! I'm done calming down! And I can tell when I'm not wanted! No one will answer my questions, Liss is gone, Brooklyn can't make up her damn mind—and what even is our relationship anyway?!

CHRIS

It's not her fault.

MATTHEW

She doesn't get it! None of them do!

CHRIS

Actually, they do. They've seen this... *obsession* before. We aren't those kids at the old man's mansion. Not anymore. And those who panic get taken away first.

MATTHEW

My God, enough with the ominous remarks already!

CHRIS

Look, man. While you were gone... this other dude came along. Kallan Jones—this tall, stupid indie guy. He... sort of took your place.

MATTHEW

Daisy—she had mentioned his name, I think.

CHRIS

Yeah, well, he was new to SBA, and since we had an extra bed, he roomed with Rhys and me while you were in Alaska. And he and Brooklyn, they just sort of... hit it off. And they dated, and they were happy. But then things got bad—Kallan got insecure or paranoid or something, and he started lashing out at Brooklyn, and it wasn't, like, healthy. At all. They broke up on prom night. And then you showed up out of nowhere.

Matthew is silent. Chris sighs.

CHRIS (cont.)

He hurt her, Matthew. Real bad. And so we're all just trying to recover from that. Everything about SBA got super serious when you left. And I'm not saying it's because of you—just that things are different now. I know things haven't turned out like they once might've. And yeah, I know you know that. But don't blame Brooklyn. She's been through a lot. It hasn't been easy.

Matthew shakes his head. He clenches his fists.

MATTHEW

Where is he?

CHRIS

Who? Kallan? (Putting his hands forward.) Man, seriously? That's in the past now.

MATTHEW

Well, obviously not, if it's still affecting the present!

Matthew stands, as does Chris.

MATTHEW (cont.)

Do you know where he is or not?

CHRIS

He's gone, Matthew! Like Liss and Pulov, he's gone. He was here for Brooklyn. Why would he stay? Why would they keep him?

MATTHEW

Who's "they"?!

> Chris waves a hand in the general direction of everywhere.
> Matthew looks around the empty room and says nothing.

CHRIS

It wasn't solely Kallan, you know. It started before him, and it's still going on now. We're here to fulfill a purpose, whether it's a diversity quota or to be the butt of a joke or to simply be a love interest to somebody. Even a suspiciously similar substitute. Of course, they don't want me to *be* black. Just look it, partially. To perform whiteness. If you can't get with the program, you're gone. Call it what you like—expelled, perma-silenced, frozen, iced... everything's always a code around here. (Crossing his arms.) You would know. We just saw you get on that bus one day, and then... Alaska.

MATTHEW

I... I have this weird feeling I'm forgetting something.

CHRIS

If anything, you're remembering too much. Of nothing.

MATTHEW

So what do we do?

CHRIS

What? There's nothing we *can* do. There's no villain, no mastermind. A societal ill, maybe...

MATTHEW

I don't believe that for a second.

CHRIS

Man, I am your best friend, and I think you should let this go. Move on. (Putting his hands in his pockets.) But if you need to talk, talk to Denzel at administration. He knows Sea Breeze Academy more than anybody. Mintz Plaza's blocked by construction for that musical number we have to do—either "Jingle Bells" or "We Wish You a Merry Christmas." So go through the tunnels Liss showed us. And hey... Matthew?

Chris hugs him.

CHRIS (cont.)

I never had a brother, but I feel like I got one with you. I love you, man.

Matthew hesitates, then hugs him back.

MATTHEW

Thanks, Chris. I'll see you soon.

CHRIS

Yeah. See you later.

Matthew steps away. He glances around the girls' lounge and settles for the door to the underground tunnels. He walks to it. He pushes on the handle and steps inside. But he looks back. From the worried look Chris gives him, it's clear the two will never see each other again, and also, from Matthew's shutting of the door and the vanishing of the light, that it's time for a commercial.

* * *

Back at Sea Breeze Academy, Matthew has followed the tunnels to the administration building. He walks around the first floor for a moment. The halls are dark, with the only light coming from behind the blinds of the windows. Matthew opens one and peers across this campus on the bluff. Grounds workers are hauling gumdrop trees, icing decorations, swirly lollipops, giant candy canes, icicle lights, holiday wreaths, stockings, presents, a terrifying tissue ghost, wooden reindeer, nutcrackers, poinsettias, and a partridge in a palm tree. More important, Virgo, Chris, and Rhys are up to their festive shenanigans.

Matthew frowns. He's about to return to the tunnels when he spots a light coming from underneath one of the doors, slightly ajar. It's labeled "Disciplinary Committee." He opens it.

The room is dimly lit. It has checkered flooring and walls made entirely of blue velvet curtains. A dozen or so teens, their legs chained to the floor, chat with one another about fat and night school and what we talk about when we talk about love. Denzel Davis, in an orange Hawaiian shirt, sits in an easy chair with his arms around Miki and another girl. Sultry jazz plays from the ceiling. In the corner, Rob Otto has been reduced to furniture.

Denzel, Miki, and the other girl laugh. He sees Matthew and waves him over.

DENZEL

Well, well, well. If it isn't Matthew, our shining star!

He holds up a bottle of expired Whazz, then drinks from it. The girls do the same.

MIKI

Just don't shut the door, 'cause it locks automatically from the outside.

MATTHEW

What's going on?

DENZEL

It's over, my dude. This is our... our end-of-the-world party.

Attached to the curtains is a sign that reads, "No Mexican flag, no strobe lights, & absolutely no depiction of Muhammad!" Matthew frowns.

DENZEL (cont.)

Oh, sorry. (Gesturing to the girl.) Matthew, this is Emma. After they fired Coach Poole for paying off the five hundred bucks Brooklyn probably stole, they were going to hire a new coach for the women's basketball team and then bring in Emma as a recruit.

EMMA

It would've been called "Emma at SBA."

DENZEL

But see, Emma's transgender, and she was gonna break a bunch of SBA records, and so you and your friends were going to debate the ethics of recruiting transgender players. Is it for diversity? Is it so the school performs better, by having someone who is built different than the other girls playing against rival schools and always winning? Of course, there'd be no definite conclusion—Emma was just gonna leave at the end of the day—'cause you can bring up social issues, sure, but don't complain or jokingly complain about anything, 'cause someone somewhere always has it worse than you. (Beat.) This was before Sea Breeze Academy decided to go in a, uh, new direction.

MATTHEW

So... Emma. You're transgender?

EMMA

Nope. I just do what they say.

MIKI

And remember, kids: owing to mechanical censorship, any ball must instead be referred to as an orb to avoid accidental vulgarity in plural forms.

EMMA

I love sucking on a sweaty pair of orbs.

DENZEL

Now you're getting it.

Denzel takes out a small baggie of cocoa snuff and scoops out a fresh, powdery mound onto his forearm. Miki hands him a plastic card, and when he's done mincing it up and separating out three brown lines, the girls and Denzel each take turns putting it under their nostrils and breathing in normally. They laugh, their noses red, the cartilage destroyed.

MATTHEW

Miki, you're talking normally.

DENZEL

Yeah, 'cause we got her out of those musty, run-down tunnels and hanging around people again. Do you know how long she was down there? Can you imagine? (Laughing.) Oh, that's right. You got Alaska, didn't you? (To the girls.) He was always eccentric, but then he started yelling about circumcision one day and how "everything's a metaphor for puberty and adulthood!" Crazy mental breakdown.

Denzel stares at Matthew, then looks back to the girls.

DENZEL (cont.)

This has all happened before. He was quickly, erm... replaced. Right, Mateo? You remember.

MATTHEW

I remember... coming back, zooming through the arctic tundra...

DENZEL

It's this school, man. Sea Breeze Academy is a complex series of pipes and mirrors. Now look at us. We're running out of stuff to say, recycling through it all.

MIKI

We're running out of stuff to say.

EMMA

Recycling through it all.

DENZEL

Coach Poole is out, Liss is out...

EMMA

I miss her. I remember her disappearing out of nowhere.

DENZEL

Hell, Daisy's gone, or she'd probably be in a throuple with us!

                    Denzel, Miki, and Emma laugh. Denzel turns to Matthew.

DENZEL (cont.)

Kallan's gone too. Like you. Maybe even because of you.

MATTHEW

I don't get it. I don't understand any of this.

DENZEL

You did this before. You meddled. And so now, your friends, they don't want you to remember—they don't want you to pull a Pulov. *Kallan* replaced *you*. Then *you* replaced *Kallan*. It's all about those performance reviews.

MATTHEW

Per... performance...?

MIKI

Awww, look at him. He's like a dog, plucked from his meadow, thrown into a dark room, shown a mirror for the first time.

EMMA

Omigosh, yeah, I know exaaaaactly what you're talking about, like, samesies, I had *the same thing*. I went through that, like, three years ago! Yeah!

MATTHEW

Stop that! Why are you all here?! Who are these extra people? What age are we, and why do I taste pennies all of a sudden? (Shaking his head.) My friends, like, instead of actually looking at the situation and giving plausible, important advice, they give... unnatural pep talks! What happened to Pulov, why are the yearbooks in the bookstore blank, and why do we resort to making fun of each other for laughs and being mean and all this pear pressure and sexual innuendos—

MIKI

Did you say, "pear pressure"?

DENZEL

Why would he say, "pear pressure"?

MIKI

That's why I'm asking!

MATTHEW

Okay, yeah, I said that, I was just hoping you'd skip over it—

DENZEL

Pear pressure! *Pear pressure!* Eat some pears, man!

EMMA

Eat 'em! Eat 'em!

> Denzel, Miki, and Emma fall back in the armchair, laughing hysterically. Denzel wipes a tear from his eye.

DENZEL

You see, Matthew? You'll miss this. Outside SBA, you're made of flesh and people can attack you. But here, you're made only of what you show people, and they can only attack what they see. The happiest people are the most ignorant. The outside air has pointed teeth. (Leaning forward.) You're *so concerned* with Pulov, aren't you? Tell me, Freckles: where in the world is Yuran?

MATTHEW

The Middle East?

DENZEL

Where in the Middle East?

MATTHEW

The… middle?

DENZEL

Nice try. You've never heard of Yuran outside this school. What do you know of Outside SBA?

MATTHEW

I… am not sure what you mean.

DENZEL

That's the problem, isn't it? You have no memories, so you replace them with what you wish for—what you long for—or maybe what you think you deserve. You and your mom and dad in a little two-story home. White walls and a blue-shingled roof, right? A golden retriever pup named Sparky. You play with your neighborhood friends. You wear the clothes Mommy buys you. You eat dinner together as a family when Daddy gets home from work. He tucks you in at night. Is that what you remember? Use your head.

MATTHEW

Brooklyn has an apple tree in her yard in Oklahoma.

DENZEL

No, Brooklyn *doesn't* have an apple tree. She doesn't even have a yard. We are conduits, and next time, you might return as someone other than yourself. Take comfort in that.

MATTHEW

My spit is red.

DENZEL

Have you been eating artificially flavored strawberry snacks?

MATTHEW

I don't remember the last time I ate anything.

MIKI

We're all a bunch of house crickets, unaware of the seasons.

EMMA

Matthew, please, give us a reason.

MIKI

Has it always been this warm in December?

EMMA

Help us.

MIKI

Help them.

EMMA

Remember.

MIKI

Grant them rest eternal.

MATTHEW

I'm sorry... I don't follow.

Miki and Emma laugh at Matthew for no good reason. They keep laughing and laughing at him. Denzel finally rolls his eyes and snaps his fingers—stopping the flow of time itself.

The jazz has cut out. Everyone is frozen but him and Matthew. Matthew takes a step back. Denzel rises and points a finger into Matthew's chest.

DENZEL

Enough of the jokes. Now I'm being serious. The questions you're asking? They're dangerous. This all disappears when the illusion is shattered. There's no coming back from that. I was fired, all right? Made fun of the school one too many times. You have to follow the rules. It's psychology one-oh-one, the law of effect. If you do this, then you get rewarded. Do that other thing, though, and you're punished, and you're in a shedload of trouble after. The individual is the refined reflection of themselves within the collective. So I'm not going to give you those answers here where there are cameras.

MATTHEW

Cameras? (Looking around.) Where?

DENZEL

Um, hello? Phones?

Denzel takes a step back.

DENZEL (cont.)

Let me introduce myself. (Holding out his hand, speaking slowly, stressing each word with increased inflection, as if to a mere child.)

Hello, my name is Denzel Davis, and I'm an investigative journalist. So if there's anything you want to *tell me*, not ask, I'll be around for a little while longer.

Matthew cautiously shakes his hand.

MATTHEW

Hi, Denzel... uhh, I want to know—wait, no. I'm *wondering* how much of this is real and how much is... something else. I look back at the simplicity of the past couple of years, and I wish we could just... rewind and pause for a while.

Denzel smiles. He touches his nose.

MATTHEW (cont.)

Huh? What is it? "Rewind and pause"?

DENZEL

Rewind and pause. Hoverboard blues. Never odd or even.

MATTHEW

Rewind and pause... rewind and pause... rewind and... oh my God. Oh my God.

The clear blue sky, yes, and the high-definition grass, and a sweeping view of the ocean, the crystal waves lapping against the shore—of course. But also the embedded marketing. The token friends. The hoverboards that will smoke but won't explode. Quirky girl glow-up. Rich kid stereotype reinforced,

reinforced. Patronizing exclusivity instead of genuine inclusivity. The sexualizing of young girls. A mob of angry kids.

Dean Fischer's office, cue postal person. There she is. Matthew watching the scene with a vaguely amused expression. Sobbing. The setting sun hot on the back of their necks. Every set of eyes in the room always, *always* settling on Matthew and Brooklyn.

To pause and rewind and play again. If it were only that simple: an unbelievable campus with its unbelievable dean and its usually well-mannered students. A low-burning anger caught in a fog of regret. All in a day at SBA. All in a day for *Sea Breeze Academy*.

DENZEL

Matthew, what are you doing this summer? Yeah? And how do you know that? Is it because you assume, because that's what's been told to you? The mind fills in the gaps. It's like when little kids keep asking *why? why?* after everything you say. Or the opposite of that. Children are curious. But us—me, Miki, Emma, your friends—we stopped asking questions a long time ago. Don't. Stop. Asking. Questions.

Denzel looks around briefly.

DENZEL (cont.)

Talk to Brooklyn. She's the answer to everything, and this time, as elusive as she can normally be, she'll talk to you. You'll find her at Redemption Rock. Last, the beginning. Lamena.

Denzel snaps his fingers. The party resumes.

Miki stands. She presents Matthew with a box of matches. He takes it, and she winks.

MIKI

Here's looking at you, you goober.

They say nothing more, and so Matthew leaves the room. He shuts the door on his way out, and then he follows the faint light to the exit doors.

He's outside. There are palm trees decorated with ornaments, and beside them, sandmen wearing straw hats and seashells for eyes. A muffled instrumental of "I'll Be Home for Christmas" plays from someplace else as Matthew begins his trek across the manicured campus. It's hard to read his face in the blinding California sunlight, and yet it's clear by his posture and steady walk that he's anticipating some long-awaited answers, and also, that it's time for a—

Well, you know how it is.

* * *

Back at Sea Breeze Academy, Brooklyn sits on a bench behind the campus chapel, situated on one of the highest bluffs, overlooking all of the school. To the right, she can see the administration building, where her mom dropped her off her first day at SBA. Chris met her then, and he gave her a tour of the places now most special to her—the food court at Mintz Plaza, their lunch spot by Zhang Hall, Matthew's dorm at Wright Suites, her own at Dutton Suites. There's Jackson Commons too, and the three lakes, and the palm-lined paths from here to there to anywhere. But it's here, at Redemption Rock behind the chapel, where she finds herself coming most days when she needs to slip away. It's here she can reflect, can meditate, in absolute peace.

Matthew steps around the red rock—more like a boulder—and sees her sitting quietly, her head bowed slightly. He waits a moment. She looks behind her, notices him, and then stares forward again, out at the school and the Pacific below. She pats the space beside her. Matthew goes over and sits.

The wind rustles through the trees around them. Matthew raises his arm to put around her, but he doesn't. She's not wearing the reindeer antlers or the scarf, and she's not dressed in that crazy lingerie from before, and she's not in that party dress from the night they shared at Dean Fischer's mansion. No, she's dressed like her normal Brooklyn self: faded blue jeans, a sleeveless crop top, high heel sneakers, and a rose heart bracelet. So why does she still look like a stranger to him?

A lone seagull soars overhead and into the horizon. Brooklyn pulls her knees to her chest. In the distance, grounds workers stomp around with their construction hats and jackhammers, their orange cones and paint, their radio chatter, as they prepare sets and scenery.

BROOKLYN

I miss the chapel bells.

MATTHEW

Me too. I'm glad we got to hear the final bongs last year.

BROOKLYN

That's some risky onomatopoeia there, bud.

MATTHEW

Ah, sorry.

BROOKLYN

No, I'm... sorry. I am sorry. I am, I am, I am.

> Brooklyn sighs.

BROOKLYN (cont.)

I have so many memories here from the past couple of years. (Pointing.) The Homecoming bonfire at Jackson Commons, where they'd have, like, a dozen firefighters on standby. Or the Fall Fair there our sophomore year. You won me that tiara. I taught you how to skip stones.

MATTHEW

(Pointing.) And Fukutsū, where we'd go for those California rolls and sashimi you love.

BROOKLYN

That's where we went when Chris needed that double date for that girl he liked.

MATTHEW

(Laughing.) And you were like, hey, pretend to be my boyfriend! And

I was all, oh yeah, sure thing, can do!

Brooklyn laughs with him. He smiles.

BROOKLYN

Remember when you, Chris, and Rhys went streaking after finals?

MATTHEW

That was a misunderstanding!

BROOKLYN

Or when the lakes turned into that swamp pit for Halloween—when there was that fake curse and those empty graves? Or the time we spent a whole day trying to get rid of Virgo's hiccups? Or! Or on my birthday last year, when you were trying to convince our friends you didn't have a crush on me, so you were, like, super mean and pretended to forget about me and... stuff. (Shaking her head.) Gaah. Sorry. I don't know why I brought that up.

MATTHEW

I was an idiot. I always liked you. (Frowning.) Brooklyn, I never stopped loving you.

She smirks.

BROOKLYN

Not sure why. I'm a total mess, and everything's wrong.

MATTHEW

Don't act like that—

BROOKLYN

I'm not acting.

> She turns her head to look at Mintz Plaza, where she
> and Matthew first met. That fountain used to run all
> the time but hasn't since the droughts. Tired grounds
> workers in coveralls polish the granite once more. The
> Mexican gardeners are hard at work in the sun.

BROOKLYN (cont.)

Look at them, tidying it all up, making SBA so pristine and picturesque.
The grass will keep growing, and they'll just keep cutting it. Like, sure, we
had our hijinks and fun, but we also used to be about community service
or empowering children or commemorating fallen veterans. Fundraising,
beach clean-ups days, studying underneath a palm tree... we used to strive
for something bigger. There must be more to this than *this*.

MATTHEW

When did we change, Rook? When was that? All our friends. SBA.
Me, somewhat, but you... but you especially. I'll be standing with you
and our friends, and I'll wonder what you're thinking, if you ever think
of me—

BROOKLYN

Of course I do. You're important to me.

MATTHEW

Please. Tell me something I know isn't made up. Give me a memory
that's real.

BROOKLYN

I really hate sushi.

> She looks over. Matthew laughs, and then Brooklyn laughs as well. But then she stops. She stops, and it's all over, and he can sense this in her dark blue eyes. Everything.

BROOKLYN (cont.)

You say that I've changed more than you have, and I agree... I have my up days and my down days. But I also know that I've seen you grow into a person who is stronger, wiser, and more sure of himself than he was at fourteen. I am so proud of you. Any girl would be so blessed to have you as her boyfriend. You never interrupt me, and you hear me, and you remember all the things I like and don't like. Hanging out with you is the coolest thing I get to do here, and I'm so glad we've gotten to do it again these past couple of weeks.

> She's crying. It's soft and hardly noticeable, but Matthew sees this, and he knows.

MATTHEW

You didn't want to date when you first got here...

> Her lower lip trembles. She begins to hyperventilate.

MATTHEW (cont.)

And you never had a boyfriend for more than a day before Kallan.

BROOKLYN

I'm... (Voice breaking.) I'm gay. I like girls, not guys, and I am so, so sorry, Matthew.

> She's crying harder, and Matthew's crying too. He puts his arm around her for real this time. She leans into him.

BROOKLYN (cont.)

And it's so hard, being a gay girl at a place like this. Because they'll fetishize you. And they won't believe you. And they think it's wrong or gross or they don't understand—and so no matter how accepting Sea Breeze Academy tries to be, I can never be openly gay when I'm at the center of attention. Can you imagine if it was Liss who's queer, or Miki? At least I'm white! Chris—he can allude to being bi whenever he sort of comments on the way a dude looks, but you never see him with a boyfriend, do you? He was with Tina for the longest time, and they didn't even really like each other all that much!

MATTHEW

Chris said we're all playing different specific parts.

BROOKLYN

And I'm the dude magnet. Everybody loves blondes, right? I'm the leader, the magnetic heroine, the fashionista girly girl with a tomboy streak... it requires so much energy. I'm trying to stay strong, but I feel overgrown. Too awake to sleep. They say I'm doing a great job, but I don't see it. I ran too much too quickly. And you and me—we're the official couple. "Will they, or won't they?" Well, they do. We do. Or did, or whatever this is. I don't know, and I don't care, and... I just want to go home.

Matthew considers what she's saying.

MATTHEW

Is there a girl?

BROOKLYN

Cass. Or Cassie. I get to see her during long breaks. We video call, and—and we write each other letters, and a couple of months back, she told me she liked me, and after I realized what she meant, I was, like... stunned. Now it's so nice being able to tell her how wonderful I think she is without feeling like I'm overstepping or anything. Matthew, it's so nice. We talk about everything. Even today, she told me again how much she liked me, and now I feel like my face is going to be red forever. I know, I know, it's so sappy and lame, but... I finally get the butterflies-in-your-stomach thing. You know—that cliché warm and fuzzy feeling when you're so relaxed and at peace with someone you really, really love...

It hurts, because it does. But this time, he understands perfectly.

MATTHEW

That's... (Taking a breath.) Pure. That's so pure, and happy. I'm happy for you. I'm sure she also... feels relieved she can be herself and express herself around you.

BROOKLYN

Sometimes I'll just sleep so the time will go by faster. But I can't sleep off this pain. What kills me is not being able to do anything. I know we only have a few more weeks here, but then... being with her is like

Christmas all the time. I feel like a little kid again. There is *nothing* for me here. I mean, no offense to anyone who likes this thing, but I'm sort of glad and silently cheering along that it's slowly walking toward its own demise. It's not fun, it's not engaging, it's not something good, and it only makes me more miserable. And yet I can't leave. So I have five hundred in cash and no way out. I don't even think the money's real. Can you imagine? Take a night train far from here and... and...

MATTHEW

You shouldn't have to do this if you don't want to.

BROOKLYN

We made a home here. A good one. But this isn't the home I want anymore.

> Brooklyn sniffs. She wipes her nose and eyes and then looks out across this same sprawling campus, flooded with sunlight.

BROOKLYN (cont.)

I hate this school. Sea Breeze Academy. I just think it's... kind of tedious? Fake? I don't know. I don't know why I keep going at it alone. But when I start to ask myself that, I also begin to ask myself why I do anything, and I'm worried that if I quit this game, I'll be quitting the reality I've dressed up for myself, and I'll spiral out of control. I'm currently at this point in my life where I feel like I need a change, and I don't really know what it is that I need. Like, I know I am stable in life and that I'm really not doing that bad, but I still feel like there is so much more I should be doing at this point, and then I get all flustered thinking about it. I'm attractive enough, smart, healthy and young, but I'm too much of a coward to quit. I'm worried that if I don't live my life the way everyone tells me to, that would also just be a lie to distract myself from my inherent lack of interest, with the added risk of accidentally falling for the lie. (Sighing.) So I go for another semester. Here's to ninety more.

> He looks at her. He really looks at her. He knows what he believes, and that's in loving someone so uncontrollably that you feel crazy like a kid. He's loved her all this time, throughout every adventure together, and he's so happy for it. And he knows what he must do, and he doesn't care where he ends up from here. And isn't it pretty to think they were strangers once, and somehow things turned in their favor, leaving him with this girl he likes so much.

MATTHEW

Brooklyn, you've always made me feel at peace. Like the things I'm scared of can't touch me, and as if the world can be what you and I make it. In crowds, or at parties, you and I are the only people in the room. Each time I look at your face, I am certain this is what it feels like to be in love.

BROOKLYN

Matthew...

MATTHEW

But enough about me—because you are a galaxy of your own. I have never met anyone like you, and I never want to, because they wouldn't do you justice. Your eyes are full of life, and when I miss you, I cling to them. You have this smile that I swear pulls me in deeper every time you laugh, and your soul is made of the most wistful and exciting parts of this universe we could ever hope to discover. I don't know if I'll ever get the words right, but you are the most beautiful person to me, and I sure do love you, Rook, with everything I have, and everything I am. So thank you for always being there for me. I'm glad we got to do this thing together.

> Here's Matthew and Brooklyn, two American kids doing whatever it takes. He kisses her cheek. She holds him tight. They sit and share this final moment together. Then Matthew stands and gently places his hand on her back so Brooklyn knows not to follow.

MATTHEW (cont.)
Merry Christmas, Brooklyn.

> She smiles faintly.

BROOKLYN
Thank you. Merry Christmas, Matthew.

> He walks away. He goes down the hills and around the grounds workers, and he doesn't stop to think about the strengthening yellow sun or the beads of sweat on his brow, about the stale breeze and the warmth radiating off his face, the carrying of it all in his peripheral vision, the heat of his body and the tightening muscles in his back and this fervor, rising into the air, free of all doubt, for once undefined by the minutes and hours

of a man-made clock. No moments of weakness. No spontaneous bouts of anxiety. Just pure concentration until he finally reaches Room 102 at Dutton Suites.

He steps inside, and he hears a whimper.

Matthew looks behind him to see Virgo crawling out of the bathroom and clutching her stomach as she holds onto the door for support. She looks out of breath. Matthew kneels beside her.

MATTHEW

Virgo? Virgo, what's wrong?

VIRGO

Nothing's...

MATTHEW

Virgo. Tell me what's wrong.

VIRGO

A year ago... I was eating a burger... and you all made a joke about me eating the burger.

Matthew sighs.

MATTHEW

I know. You're right. I did do that. And that was wrong of me. Virgo, I'm... so sorry.

VIRGO

Nobody wants... a fat roommate.

Matthew helps Virgo to her feet. She stumbles forward. He picks her up.

MATTHEW

I'm going to fix this. For you, for us. We're gonna get you back to your family. All right? Hey—do you understand? Stay with me, Virgo.

She nods slowly, then grimaces from the pain.

MATTHEW (cont.)

Find Brooklyn. Find her, Chris, and Rhys. Find anyone who's still left. Get as far away from Dutton Suites as you can. Okay?

VIRGO

Okay, but… they might be watching… and… and what are you doing…?

MATTHEW

I'm sending us home.

VIRGO

So you know… about Sea Breeze Academy.

MATTHEW

Yes. Now go.

VIRGO

I didn't want it to be true… didn't want to ruin what little time we had left…

She hesitates. Matthew remembers her as the girl from two years ago wearing feathers in her hair and tutus over her jeans. Now she's matured and not as carefree with her outfits. She's been stretched thin—that's apparent to him now. Why didn't he notice before, that actions have consequences? She deserves support, not this.

Virgo holds her gaze on him for some time before leaving. He stays a minute after her. Then he takes out the matches.

Matthew rummages through the drawers of Room 102. He tosses aside movie ticket stubs, campus brochures, birthday cards, old homework assignments, photo booth pictures, silly notes, scripts, and miscellaneous papers onto the floor, and then he gathers these items into a pile. Then he lights a match. And he drops it.

A glowing red spot emerges. A wisp of smoke rises. The razor-tipped flames climb high, and they engulf the room, dancing around these pieces of their past, Matthew sitting in the middle of it all, his legs crossed, his body finally relaxed.

Goodbye to the boys-versus-girls antics, the comebacks, the pranks. The dates, the drama, the mess ups, the break ups. Matthew can think of a whole montage of the crazy fun he's had here: food fights, talent shows, elections, dance competitions, haunted houses, and Springfest each year. When the gang got detention together, or when a stray dog ate their research report. When the gang came up with an idea to stop dolphin bycatch for a science contest and won a marine life sight-seeing trip. When emergency drills kept getting in the way of him asking out Brooklyn. When Virgo started an advice segment on *SBA News*. When Liss tried to prove she could be a bad girl, and when Rhys started rating people on a schoolwide popularity list. When Rhys got in trouble for it. When Miki took Rhys on a date to Fukutsū, or the time a squirrel chased Chris up a tree. The day Liss almost killed Nurse Morgan with a catapult and slime. Coach Poole with his megaphone, Sage with her wisdom, Daisy with her good looks, and Denzel with his charm. When they all made a tranquility garden outside Zhang Hall. When they all got sick with the flu. Kite-flying. Beach parties. Beginnings. Endings.

They first try the door handle, then start kicking at the door itself. By the time it gives, the fire has already spread to other rooms and is just starting to leap across buildings and scorch the lawn between.

The grounds workers drag Matthew out by the arms and throw him onto the grass. He's coughing out of instinct, but he likes the smell. The workers are busy with the chaos. The sirens blare like the cries of a hoarse man, of a soft-spoken man, of a stern woman— all frantically screaming for a way out. Matthew smiles to himself. In his mind, he imitates the sound.

The workers are soon followed by the men in suits and ties. Dean Fischer runs over to Dutton Suites, and he's yelling at people, and his hair is more noticeably gray today, and he is beyond furious.

Firetrucks drive up from the Pacific Coast Highway.

Students are scurrying, and they quickly abandon their SBA backpacks in an attempt to run faster. The teens stampede each other and cry and film with their phones and shout out panicked conjectures. Nurse Morgan is trampling about with a jar of pickle juice. The Men Against Women Protesting protestors are back for some reason. The men in suits approach them.

Dean Fischer steps slowly toward Matthew. He looks disappointed but not surprised.

DEAN FISCHER

I warned you to stay out of the way. You prioritized your own confusion and fear over the concern of others.

MATTHEW

(Coughing.) You… you want to burn with the school, be my guest.

DEAN FISCHER

Dammit, kid. Why this? Why now?

There's an explosion from behind. They look. Warm air blasts against their faces, then ash, then gray sky. Dean Fischer's tie is flapping in the dry and angry wind. He turns to Matthew.

DEAN FISCHER (cont.)

You sought to break what you labeled as routine. But if we find purpose in that which is purposeless, why challenge it? Why should you determine what is valueless? We all have a part to play here—you know that.

MATTHEW

And what about you, Dean Fischer? What about Pulov and Brooklyn? What's your role?

> The dean kicks Matthew hard in the side. Matthew sputters, coughing up spit and blood. The dean frowns.

DEAN FISCHER

I'm the authority figure.

> The men in suits remove Matthew from the ground and carry him off. He twists his neck to catch another glimpse of the dean, but Dean Fischer's too busy with the reds and yellows and riots to pay Matthew any attention. Matthew hits his head on something. It's the bumper of an SBA utility van. The men open the back doors and haul him in. The smoke in the air is thick and starting to pixelate. They shut the doors and lock it.
>
> Matthew bangs his fists against the inside walls of the van as it lurches away from campus. They must be driving over debris, as each bump in the road is bigger than the last, sending Matthew rocking back and forth as the air gets harder to breathe. He remembers soccer balls. He remembers duck, duck, goose and tag. He dreams of having dreamed his dreams, hoping that he would find a day to ask what he could see. But they are shapes. Just shapes. Without life or meaning.
>
> And then everything is white.
>
> The van is gone.
>
> The school is dissolved.

The world is quiet.

And Matthew descends. And Matthew descends. Everything spins, and he drops, and he lessens, lessens, lessons.

It is due to a collective human aggregation that we are able to create things of deniably and undeniably inherent nature that would have otherwise surfaced in some other medium and probably not as clearly. Creation is the space in which we are woven. The act of creating is a channel from that space.

There is Matthew, falling hopelessly, starving for all eternity, trapped in ice like a beautiful sculpture, still conscious. This isn't even death. A quiet voice humming in the background to a tuneless melody. A liminal space devoid of God's light. A frigid, horrible pocket of unbearable cold.

Nothing. Empty.

1. Hey Brando, shut that off.

...

2. OK it's off.

1. Thanks bud.

"DREAMBOAT WEEKEND"

As their semester comes to a close, the gang reminisce on a year full of memories and look forward to the adventures that await them.

A nother perfect day in Southern California, and Sea Breeze Academy is burning to the ground. The sky is a bitter orange, and the row after row of buildings are black and disintegrating. The ocean air fans the flames: fire, everywhere; fire, everything; boy and girl and sea between.

Flying away from campus is a twin-engine private helicopter. Inside are Brooklyn, Virgo, Chris, Rhys, and Siddiq. Virgo and Rhys are watching the chaos on their side, while Chris and Siddiq silently hold hands. Brooklyn sits in the middle, her back against the leather seating, her elbow crammed against a coffee machine. She rubs her head. She tries to relax in the warmth of the sun but can't.

The surf sounds loudly over the chaos below. They fly past oceanfront mansions, sailboats, docks, and twenty-one miles of scenic beauty receding into the distance. Safe off the coast is a full-sized, multi-deck, 210-foot white yacht with a hot tub, helipad, and an American flag on the rear. Rhys points to it.

RHYS

Okay, yacht rules: if you get motion sickness, go to the front of the yacht. Don't drop your phone in the water while trying to get pics. Same with sunglasses. And if there are two of you together and we hit an iceberg, share the door. You can both survive.

VIRGO

An iceberg? Here?

CHRIS

Man, what are we going to do? SBA is... is gone.

RHYS

SBA? You mean the Sunshine Institute? (Laughing.) It's fine, all right? The board of directors'll collect the insurance money, maybe build a digital representation—something like a one-to-one scale model replica—I don't know, just don't be so depressing, jeez. My mom was nice enough to let you dudes spend the weekend on our yacht while she's away. Just enjoy it, you know?

VIRGO

She's no stage mom, that's for sure.

> The helicopter lands on the *Nielsen*, which features gold fittings on the railings, anchor, and porthole rims, as well as vibrant neon pink lightbars on the yacht's exterior. Rhys, Virgo, Chris, Siddiq, and Brooklyn exit the chopper and sit in the lounge chairs by the hot tub on the sundeck, where a stereo plays royalty-free house music. The yacht is large and luxurious. They face

away from the shoreline.

Virgo takes off her clothes until she's in her tan lace bra and underwear. Floral bangles slide up and down her thin wrists as she moves into the hot tub with Rhys, who's shirtless in his board shorts and has a patchwork of scars on his back. Brooklyn sees that the makeup covering her hibiscus flower tattoo rubbed off at some point in all the commotion. She puts two fingers on the flower and then closes her eyes. She breathes in through the nose, out through the mouth. She takes off her pants.

Chris, still wearing his polo shirt, joins Brooklyn, Virgo, and Rhys in the hot tub. Siddiq leaves for one of the bathrooms in the guest suites below deck.

VIRGO (cont.)

Hey, whose foot is that?

RHYS

Whose foot do you want it to be?

Virgo splashes Rhys in the face. He smiles as he pushes his hair back.

VIRGO

So there's this event going on right now to stand on the beach and protest the wildfires.

BROOKLYN

Please tell me you're joking.

CHRIS

Seriously? Do they expect the fire to stop and apologize? Like, I'm proud of the activism, but I don't think the flames are gonna listen.

BROOKLYN

I don't know whether to laugh or cry.

RHYS

Naw, dude, this is good, this is all good. Everything dies. Think of all the free time we'll have now. I wanna get my own show on some food network's morning block—you know the ones. Where the kitchen's eerily clean, and the host is always smiling, and sometimes they invite their friends and relatives, and every episode ends with a garden party and a pitcher of sangria. Nothing stressful like *Raise the Steaks*. No way.

BROOKLYN

There certainly is a gap in the market.

VIRGO

Don't even say anything. Just sit and stare at the camera while eating food with no expression. Eat it slowly.

RHYS

Yeah, and I'll be crying for no reason, and then I'll just end it with, "It was good, yeah... yeah, it was good. It was okay. It's all fine." And then the camera falls or something.

> Seagulls screech in the distance. Brooklyn grits her teeth and blinks back tears, the sun on her shoulders, the ocean breeze in her blonde hair.

CHRIS

So...

BROOKLYN

So.

RHYS

So?

CHRIS

Biggest regrets?

BROOKLYN

Most friendships with boys.

VIRGO

Stressing over me eating way too much. Me thinking my raccoon-eyed makeup and lime green skinny pants looked *great* on me our ninth-grade year. Or the first time I had a panic attack and didn't really understand what was happening.

RHYS

Not keeping up with my daily workout routine.

CHRIS

Probably what happened to Miki the first time. I remember shunning her for lying over something super trivial, and two weeks later, Australia. Let me tell you, I do not hold grudges anymore.

BROOKLYN

Being too trusting, opening up too much about my personal life, and exposing myself emotionally to complete strangers because I thought they were my friends.

VIRGO

Or, for me, not socializing enough, not being more intentional with people. Wish I'd thought more seriously about my future and put more effort into making and strengthening friendships with people I actually wanted to be friends with.

RHYS

Matthew destroying all his friendships at once because of paranoia and spite.

BROOKLYN

Hey, knock it off. Don't talk about Matthew like that.

RHYS

Matthew? Who's Matthew? General Blah? (Laughing.) I'm joking.

VIRGO

Yeah, but who *was* Matthew really? What lies beneath the facade?

BROOKLYN

Matthew was... a good guy. He put others before himself.

RHYS

Yeah, if it was a firing squad.

CHRIS

Dude!

RHYS

Oh, come on! Matthew was a total snake! He was creepy, he was downright *stalkerish* to Brooklyn in the early days, and he was obsessed with the negative attention his complaining got him! Like, oh yes, Matthew, you are the *most* broken and the *most* messed-up person ever *in the world!* Please. People have been through a lot more than him and they kept it moving. He needed to stop trying to be so edgy. Brooklyn—remember all the times he would sneak in through your window?

VIRGO

Dude. Be nice. Salt is for food, not attitudes. (Rolling her eyes.) You know what? I'm just gonna say it: food is good.

CHRIS

Food never hurt my feelings.

RHYS

Except now it's like, oh, you like food, don't you? Well, guess what? Food is *cancelled!*

BROOKLYN

Seems accurate.

RHYS

It's like we say every single time: it's okay, hope you feel better, your feelings are valid! And yet he ignores every one of our suggestions!

(Crossing his arms.) Less introspective and curious than he was sad and pathetic.

CHRIS

They say the more intelligent an animal is, the more capable they are of destruction. Sometimes including the destruction of themselves, if basic needs aren't being met. Like, parrots are pretty well known for their tendency of self-destruction when they get neglected or upset. (Beat.) I philosophate sometimes.

BROOKLYN

No, it's… for him, it was too late to unlearn it. It's like you're exposed to the same environment over and over, so your mind adapts to it, but it feels wrong and not actually you, and so once you're in a different environment, it's too late. Like when you have a plant that grows crooked because it's too far from the window, and then you bring it out, and it starts straightening. I guess the only way to deal with it is to wait for you to grow beyond the growth pattern you were constricted to. I mean, it takes time, but the plant eventually fixes itself. It's not like things will be completely reverted… but they'll eventually wear off, mostly.

VIRGO

I miss Matthew. I miss Liss. We never did find out if "Liss" was short for "Melissa" or "Felicity."

CHRIS

Rats aren't even weird pets. You know what's a weird pet to have?

VIRGO

A flamingo.

CHRIS

Even if someone had a flamingo, I wouldn't bring them down for it. I'd be like, whoa, cool flamingo.

BROOKLYN

Okay, so I change my answer. My biggest regret is pretty much everything I've ever said and done.

Virgo smiles.

VIRGO

I'm sorry, but are you me?

CHRIS

(Smiling.) Are you me as well?

RHYS

Are we all the same person?

BROOKLYN

When did I enter this house of mirrors?

RHYS

Why aren't mirrors made of ice when we can feel it?

CHRIS

Why isn't ice made out of mirrors when we *can't* feel it?

VIRGO

Is quartz wild glass or is glass domesticated quartz?

BROOKLYN

Asking the important questions.

VIRGO

In all seriousness though, SBA has gotten pretty strict about us talking about our feelings, so... maybe we should stop? Like, I was talking about loneliness to you, Brooklyn, a couple of days ago and—

BROOKLYN

I think it's 'cause loneliness can be related to depression, and that topic's not allowed here anymore.

CHRIS

We're not allowed to feel anything but the happiness we're forced to keep up.

RHYS

All smiles all the time.

VIRGO

It's weird. Sometimes I'm blatantly talking about my depression and they won't care, then other times I just say, "I'm sad and it's raining today," and they act fast. So who knows.

BROOKLYN

It all depends on what exactly you're saying and how you're saying it. Like how you can talk about SeaBreezeAcademy dot com, but you can't talk about websites other than that.

CHRIS

There's no consistency. They can choose to strike you down or spare you depending on their mood. It basically boils down to trying to stay on their good side.

BROOKLYN

But it goes beyond that! For example: there was this really interesting conversation happening at Mintz Plaza the other day about veganism and how people and corporations can or should be more eco-friendly. I didn't see anything harmful about the subject matter—didn't hear any insults or whatever—but the men in suits came anyway! I hate how anything intellectual gets removed right away.

CHRIS

They don't like real-world topics.

RHYS

Some massive propaganda operation.

BROOKLYN

They're dumbing us down is what they're doing.

VIRGO

I can understand how certain topics would cause major issues and not be okay to have in a setting where there are kids and teenagers. But when everyone is being civil and just talking about the potential benefits of veganism or how society should be better to the environment, then yeah, that should be allowed. I'm not even vegan and I don't want to

356 BRYANT A. LONEY

be, but it still sounds interesting!

BROOKLYN

Right?

RHYS

So, what, we're just going to admit everything we've wanted to say before but couldn't?

Virgo stands.

VIRGO

I buy expensive water to raise my social standing!

Chris claps to this.

RHYS

Whoa, does that work?

Virgo glares at Rhys, then sits back down.

VIRGO

Yes, I am constantly looked up to, and my pretend wealth is coveted by many.

RHYS

Yeah, well, all Lita Candyce songs sound like they were written by some thirteen-year-old.

VIRGO

I want to like her music, and I do in theory, but… no offense, Chris, but most of it's boring.

CHRIS

None taken. I'm going to sound like a total hipster-moron, but I'm really not a fan of her newer stuff. She's collaborating with rappers now, and it just doesn't feel right.

BROOKLYN

She's not one of my favorite artists or anything, but I'm glad she exists.

RHYS

Last thing I'll say about Matthew: haven't you noticed that every time you express being upset with his behavior, he only pushes the boundaries more and more? Brooklyn, you were right to cut ties with him. He wasn't your responsibility. You did what's best for you.

VIRGO

And now I get to visit home, and Brooklyn gets to see… what was her name? Cassie?

RHYS

Well, I don't get to go anywhere.

CHRIS

What do you mean?

RHYS

What? I mean what I mean. I'm not going anywhere. This is it.

BROOKLYN

Huh. Maybe you're right.

> Brooklyn and Chris exchange a look, as if they're trying to remember something they purposefully forgot.

VIRGO

I'm worried about the flooding though. That's all I hear when people mention Peru—the floods, the rain, gaah. They're my family, you know?

RHYS

But we're your family. Here, at SBA.

VIRGO

I... suppose. (Shaking her head.) Anyway, I think I'm done tubbing. Where are the showers?

RHYS

Here, I'll show you.

> Rhys and Virgo exit the hot tub, with Rhys giving Chris a suggestive eyebrow raise as he walks Virgo inside the yacht.
>
> Chris looks to Brooklyn, then scratches at his new stubble as he too gets out. Brooklyn picks up a towel from one of the chairs and starts drying off. She takes her time, her body cold and rigid.
>
> The sun has set over the turbulent waves. The stars are out and quivering, almost terrifyingly dark. Brooklyn remembers a night last spring when she and

Matthew had lain in the grass beside one of the lakes, and he had made up crazy stories for each constellation she'd pretended to find. She had laughed and laughed after each one because he was funny and a natural storyteller, even in his rambling. He had a bright imagination, and he wasn't any of what Rhys had gone on about. Matthew was a good friend. A great one. She misses him. She wishes she could recall one of those stories of his.

And so she wonders: was it worth it?

Siddiq returns with cocoa snuff on his upper lip. He chats briefly with Chris. Brooklyn leans against the railing, looking out over the water and the heavy black night—at the paper moon and cardboard sea. The coast is growing fainter by the minute, though she can still see the show-stopping blaze. Siddiq sits on one of the lounge chairs farther off, and Chris joins Brooklyn at the side of the *Nielsen*.

The wind picks up, a faint tang of burning. Chris rubs the back of his neck.

CHRIS

Hey. How are you holding up?

BROOKLYN

So, so. I have this goodbye anxiety, this… this feeling of being unfinished. I've been awake for four days now. (Glancing over at Siddiq.) He's quiet.

CHRIS

Yeah. Sorry. Siddiq's shy around people he doesn't know too well.

BROOKLYN

It's been years.

CHRIS

I know, I know. He used to talk. A lot. Now he has to force himself to say anything at all. He just doesn't have anything to say anymore. (Sighing.) I never want to be that quiet.

BROOKLYN

I thought this would feel different, that'd I'd be happy for once. But I'm not. I don't. I feel…

CHRIS

Empty?

BROOKLYN

I sometimes feel as if I gave birth to this place.

> The *Nielsen* moves slowly but surely. At the bow up front, it cuts effortlessly through the water. But behind, at the stern, the yacht leaves discord and severance in its path, creating violent waves of white, drifting on its own reflection.

BROOKLYN (cont.)

It's nice imagining we have a life outside here.

CHRIS

You mean with Virgo talking about her family in Peru. (Crossing his arms.) Or you with Cassie.

BROOKLYN

Whatever we want most—that's what keeps us going, keeps us motivated to soldier through. Possibilities. A more peaceful life.

CHRIS

Matthew couldn't picture anything else, you know. We were what he wanted. This was home.

> She looks up at the stars, distant and dying. She grips the railing.

BROOKLYN

It's frustrating having these narrative expectations. All our lives we want answers—when will this happen, what is that, who are they, do you smell something burning, you name it. And everyone avoids the questions! Never do we actually get the response we're hoping for. The answers in our head are far superior to whatever they, to whatever I, could come up with. So they leave it to you to figure out. "And where's the fun in that?" you say. And someone else replies, "You tell me."

CHRIS

He's been gone before. Matthew.

BROOKLYN

This is different. It doesn't feel good.

CHRIS

Where in a cycle does culpability belong?

BROOKLYN

Do you ever get those odd dreams... not nightmares, but about people you've forgotten about, but who your stupid dreams refuse to let you forget, and it leaves you with a sort of... a sort of dream hangover? And then the residual feelings the following day are... are...

>   Chris takes off his eyepatch. He turns it over in his
>   hands.

CHRIS

Are not nice.

BROOKLYN

Right. It makes me sad and brings back these regrets. Like, I'd rather have nightmares than these ancient dreams. They're not even people I know. They're people I'll dream about with no idea who they were— just that I miss them like they were a part of me.

CHRIS

Your brain can't make up new faces. Everyone you've dreamed of, you've seen in your life at one point or another, even if it's just a mashup of features. It'll sometimes be this person from your past, but it won't really be them at all.

BROOKLYN

The people not being real just makes the feelings that much stronger. Real-life people have their own agendas. Real people are disappointing.

CHRIS

Only if you don't accept them and love them for who they are.

BROOKLYN

Lame.

CHRIS

Lamena?

> Lamena. A fish. From the lakes and rivers of Madagascar. Lamena. A small village in the eastern region of Burgundy, France. Lamena. A girl's name, to be creative. It's a nonsense word. Lamena has no purpose, no part to play.
>
> Brooklyn takes in the dark of the ocean and the night's black nothingness, and the little blue torch in each of her eyes light up: it's not the end of the world after all. Just today. Tonight, she can rest.

BROOKLYN

Yes. Lamena.

> She looks in the direction of the beach, where crickets whisper their nightly passions while the tide stands still, prying on private lives and parts. These Gryllidae are neither proud nor shy nor even excited, but they are content with their evenings, not staged but a stage. It is written in their music. It is a song they produce by moonlight, the glow of the campus in the distance. They rub against each other, the naked grandeur of

their hairy legs—chk chk, chk chk, chk chk, chk chk. Wings up and open, acoustical sails. Not only these two, but a twelve million sum spread across the sound of a steady summer. They are the gatekeepers to a good night's sleep, to a mutual pleasure. They do not ask for more than they can give, no secrets for themselves. They lather in the other's voice, one quieter, one with the charm of a rambling man. Subtle variations in their speech. And if they squint, well, they can see Orion. Just past the horizon there. Slightly right of center.

THE END